THE MARRIAGE BRIBE
A Grumpy/Sunshine Marriage of Convenience Love Story
by
Amber Cross

The Marriage Bribe

A Covered Bridge Romance, Volume 1

Amber Cross

Published by Amber Cross, 2024.

This is a work of fiction. Similarities to real people, places, or events are entirely coincidental.

THE MARRIAGE BRIBE

First edition. November 20, 2024.

Copyright © 2024 Amber Cross.

ISBN: 979-8227640147

Written by Amber Cross.

Chapter One

"Act natural. Just be yourself."

If he had a dime for every time the director with her bleached teeth and silicone breasts said that to the contestants, Logan Shaw wouldn't be moonlighting as a security guard for this reality tv show.

"Whadya think?" Chris Cote asked, coming to stand beside him.

"Of the Christmas trees?" Evergreens transforming the back dining room into a winter wonderland during this dry, brown season had been furnished by the Cote Tree Farm.

"Nah. Them." Chris waved a hand at the twenty-five women draped over the furniture. "Think any of them will go through with it?"

"Maybe a few." Logan shrugged. "But live with him for six months afterwards?"

"Right. Are the men here yet?"

"Any minute now. Twenty-five *true locals* being flown in from out of state."

They both smirked.

"Okay, ladies," the director shouted through her megaphone, though her sharp voice carried easily to all four corners of the room. "They're coming." She clasped a headset to her ear, nodded once, and shouted, "Remember. Act natural. Just be yourself."

Logan took up his position beside the lobby doors while the women preened, some reaching inside their gowns to plump their breasts, others dangling a bare leg outside a long slit in their skirts. The

Ditz Brigade, as Chris had dubbed the four staying in one of his family's rental cabins, moved away from the main group and claimed a corner of the room.

The tall one lowered herself to the windowsill. The one with a hem made of ribbons bent her knee and placed her foot on the boot rail of the mini-bar to show off a long leg. The curvy one stretched her arm across the back of a bookcase and twisted her hips at a flattering angle, and the short one with the high neckline perched on top of a tall barstool.

"Good luck, buddy." Chris clapped him on the shoulder and made his way to the rear exit, adding over his shoulder, "It's gonna be a long month."

Logan laughed. "Get out of here before they think you're one of the available men."

HE WASN'T LAUGHING four weeks later.

He should have been celebrating, with the reality show done filming and the last of the cast and crew scheduled to fly out by the end of the weekend.

Instead, he was trying hard to drink away the sight of his kid brother's body being lowered into a rectangular hole in the ground. Trying to ignore the absence of their mother at the graveside service, something that still had the power to hurt him even after all the years of neglect she'd shown them.

"Why'd she call me Dummer?"

His brother had been five years old when he asked that question, exposed for the first time to kids making fun of his given name in kindergarten class.

"She always loved Fort Dummer State Park," Logan lied. He couldn't look into those innocent blue eyes and explain that he was the product of a one-night stand at the Vermont campground, much like he was the result of a weekend at North Carolina's Lake Logan.

His phone lit up where it was plugged into the wall socket by his chair.

"*How are you doing?*" Ivy asked.

A question he had heard from several people over the last week, yet he was no closer to forming a reply now than he had been then. How could he explain the devastation of learning that the seizures Dummer had been experiencing were finally identified as signs of something much darker, and uglier. They barely had time to process the diagnosis when he was gone. Just like that, his life snuffed out six weeks before his eighteenth birthday. Six weeks before they could finally live together as a family.

"*Please answer my text and let me know you're alright.*" This time it was Lauren.

But he wasn't. The screen went black and all he could see was his brother's onyx headstone. What should the inscription say? the mason had asked. Logan didn't know how to answer. How could he possibly capture everything Dummer Shaw had been, had promised to be, in a line or two?

In the end he had settled for, "Beloved brother. Gone too soon."

His phone lit up again. Chris, this time.

"*Hey, buddy, just checking in.*"

Genuine messages of concern from his closest friends, but he couldn't talk right now so he turned his phone over and took a long swallow of beer.

He rarely drank the stuff. Being co-owner of Above the Notch restaurant meant he had access to top shelf liquor, but he didn't want the staff to know he was drowning himself in alcohol tonight. Or any night, really; he had worked hard to earn, and protect, his reputation.

For Dummer's sake.

Maybe he should call someone, after all. Misery likes company and all of that.

Instead, he dragged himself out of his gaming chair, currently his sole piece of living room furniture, and went to the fridge for another beer. He was pulling a can free of the plastic webbing when someone knocked on the door.

It had to be a female; none of his male friends knocked.

Whoever it was would be sorry they came because even while he contemplated reaching out to someone, he would be lousy company tonight. He planned to finish this six-pack, have another, maybe even a third one after that, and pass out on his unmade mattress.

The knock came again.

He kicked the refrigerator door closed and popped the can open with his thumb. Chugging half the beer down in one gulp, he flipped on the outside light switch and looked through the window to see who his visitor was.

Of all the people he thought might be on the stoop outside his second story apartment, the shortest member of the *Ditz Brigade* wasn't one of them. He opened the door just enough to bark, "Is something wrong with Chris?"

"No."

He closed the door in her face and went back to his chair. Resting the beer between his legs, he picked up the gaming console and started playing a futuristic adventure challenge on his wall-mounted television screen. Pure escapism.

She knocked again and he turned up the volume. The action scene was loud. If she knocked a third time, he wouldn't hear it.

"I came to see you."

"Arrgh!" He all but jumped out of his chair, beer falling sideways in his lap and spilling onto his jeans-clad thigh. He kept his wits enough to hold the console out of the way, but now he had one more thing to be angry about, and now his anger had a target.

"What the hell are you doing here?" Standing, he advanced on her where she stood just inside the apartment. At six feet tall he towered over her much lesser height, but she didn't back away. That only made him angrier. "Did it look like I was inviting you in?"

"No."

"Because I wasn't. Go away."

"I want to talk to you."

"Then it sucks to be you, because I don't want to talk." He didn't even know the girl's name. She was *Super Ditz*, as opposed to simply ditz. In his head he used that name to distinguish her from the others.

"Just hear me out."

"Nothing you say could interest me." Her voice alone grated on his already strung-out nerves; the airy-fairy sound of it, soft and high pitched like a little girl. He slurped some beer from the can in his hand and belched. Loudly. Deliberately. "Nothing about you interests me."

That was a direct hit. He could tell by the way she flinched, but she regrouped almost immediately. Forehead pleating between slanted brows, a resolute look on her elfin face, she forged ahead. "I think you'll be interested in the proposition I have for you."

"Only if you're offering to get naked," he smirked, swallowing the rest of his beer and tossing the can behind him. Over his shoulder without even looking to see where it might land. Her brown eyes went wide. Enjoying her reaction to the caveman act, he leaned in close enough for her to get a waft of beer-laden breath and added, "Not gonna lie. I could really use some mindless sex tonight."

She seemed lost for words. That was a no, then.

Turning away, he opened the refrigerator and pulled another can of beer from its plastic webbing. He popped the top open and drank several swallows while holding the door ajar with his foot. That way he could finish this one and immediately go for the next.

He hadn't forgotten her. He just hoped if he ignored her, she would go away.

No such luck. She inhaled, a deep breath probably meant to give her courage, and said, "What if I offered you money for a down payment on that house you want?"

His hand paused midway to his mouth. Everyone knew he worked around the clock. To support this town that had supported him since he came here as an angry and confused foster child. To provide a home for himself and Dummer, a place where they could finally live together as a family. Apparently people on the film set thought he was doing it for the money.

Super Ditz mistook his stillness for interest and pressed on. "Even though the show is over and didn't end up like they wanted, the sponsors are making good on their offer. I guess they want to avoid a lawsuit." She giggled, though it wasn't funny.

Was she nervous? She ought to be.

"I get a twenty thousand dollar check the day I marry and another hundred six months later if I'm still married to, and living with, my local husband."

He looked at her now. Glared at her for rubbing salt in his open wounds, but she was either too dense, or too self-absorbed, to see the fury building inside him.

"If you marry me, I'll give you five grand toward the house you want to buy."

He put his beer down on the counter, kicked the refrigerator door shut and stomped toward her. She took a step back, then stopped and stood her ground.

He might have admired her bravado if she hadn't just insulted him with her gigolo offer.

"No."

She ignored the finality of that one-word reply. "But it would be the perfect solution for both of us," she explained. "You get the house. I get the money I need. And since you don't like me, there wouldn't be any reason for the divorce to be complicated."

Not *like* her? He despised everything about her. Yet he had a feeling she would just argue more if he said that, so instead he leaned in close enough for his end-of-day whiskers to scrape against her cheek and hissed in her ear, "I get fifty percent or no deal."

Her mouth fell open at his counteroffer, and he used that moment of surprise to physically remove her from his apartment. Taking her arm, he led her out onto the stoop, stepped back inside, and shut the door in her face. This time he flipped the lock and pulled the curtain over the window.

It was raining outside. She could either stand there and get wet or leave. He turned off the outside light to help her with that decision.

"Seven-point-five," she yelled from the other side of the panel.

He went to the fridge for another beer.

"Okay, I'll give you eight."

He was amazed. First, that she was still there, in the dark, in the rain, and second, that he could hear her over that rain. How her wispy little girl voice penetrated a steady downpour was beyond him.

Popping the can open, he settled back into his gaming chair and picked up the controller. This was the first Friday night he'd been home in weeks, and he wanted nothing more than to play video games and get so drunk he'd forget the last seven days, the last ten years, the loss that was tearing him up inside.

"Eight and a half?"

He licked the foam off his knuckles and took a big swallow of beer. Maybe she didn't understand him when he said nothing about her interested him. He had no time for women who traded on their looks for money. He'd had enough of the contestants with their heavy makeup and slinky dresses. Their ridiculous high heels had no place in northern New Hampshire. He wanted his life, and his town, back.

Footsteps retreated down the outside staircase. The rain tapered off.

He shouldn't get up. He needed this six-pack, and the next, and he had a right to drink them in his apartment without interruption.

Yet he didn't hear an engine. No headlights flashed across the living room window.

Was *Super Ditz* walking back to Cote's tree farm in this weather? It was early November, cold as well as wet, and a good three miles to the cabin from his apartment.

"Dammit all," he growled, because he could no more let her wander around town in the dark than he could ignore someone stranded on the side of the road with a flat tire.

Tossing the controller aside, he heaved himself up out of the gaming chair and stalked to the door. When he flipped on the outside light and pulled the curtain aside, there was no one in the yard below. The single streetlight at the corner reflected on an empty stretch of wet pavement leading toward town.

Cursing again, he grabbed his keys from the counter and slammed out of the apartment.

He'd give her a ride. Just take her back to her cabin and good riddance to her after that.

In his angry haste he tripped on the last stair tread. His feet hit the slick surface and went out from under him so fast he didn't have time to brace for the fall. Slam! His back bounced off the wooden treads. Slam! A second hit before he came to rest at the bottom with his butt in a puddle and his temper soaring.

This time tomorrow he would have purple welts across his spine. Her fault. If she hadn't shown up, uninvited, he'd be finishing his first six pack and racking up points in his video game. Her fault, again.

By the time he found her slogging her way up the hill out of town, he was loaded for bear. Rolling down the window, he yelled, "Get in the truck!"

She jumped. Not jumped, as in hurried to obey. That would be too easy. Instead, she backed away from the vehicle and looked nervously in both directions, almost as if she thought she could outrun him.

He put the window up, threw the truck into park and got out. In the glare of the headlights her eyes widened, and he realized she probably hadn't recognized him until now.

"So help me, if you say one word, I'll leave you here to drown in the gutter," he snarled, yanking the passenger door open. By now his clothing was soaked through and he was regretting the impulse that brought him out of his warm, dry apartment.

She took another step back. "You've been drinking. I don't ride with people under the influence."

Not completely stupid, after all. At another time he might comment on the wisdom of that reply, but just then a gust of icy wind barreled down the road and drenched him stone cold sober.

"Fine." He slammed the passenger door shut. "Suit yourself."

Rounding the front of the truck, he got in and grimaced when his clothes squished as he settled into the driver's seat. Seeing her dripping on the side of the road didn't even make him feel better. In fact, it spiked his temper to almost volcanic levels.

He rolled the window down again and called out, "Last chance."

In reply, she started walking up the hill away from him.

He threw the truck into drive and followed her.

At the top of the hill, she stopped. He shifted into park. She opened the truck door and asked," How much do you weigh?"

"What?"

"How much do you weigh, and how many beers have you had?"

"One eighty, and four cans. No, three and a half, since you made me spill most of one." Technically, the fourth one was barely touched, sitting opened next to his gaming chair where he left it to come check on her. Irritated all over again, he barked, "Are you getting in or not?"

She scrunched up her face, bit her lip, then with a pained look on her face, climbed into the cab. "Thank you."

"Not. One. Word."

Chapter Two

Well, that could have gone better, Prissy lamented as she peeled off her sodden clothes and dropped them on the bathroom floor with a splat.

She hadn't gone into this without doing her homework. For weeks she'd watched Logan Shaw on the film set, the careless playboy who had all the women in the room swooning with one flash of his blue eyes, one quirk of a dark eyebrow. They gushed about how they'd like to have the part-time security guard frisk them. He was handsome as sin, but he was also thoroughly disagreeable. Every time he looked at her, his expression bordered on revulsion.

That made him a good candidate for her proposal.

She didn't care why he treated her like gum on his shoe. It might have bothered her once. Not now. With a ticking financial time bomb set to go off in a matter of days, she was desperate.

She hadn't slept a full night since concluding that none of the male contestants would ask for her hand in marriage and she had no chance of getting the payout. Then the girls in her cabin said Logan was moonlighting for extra money and a spark of hope penetrated the dark cloud hanging over her.

He was local. He didn't like her. Five thousand dollars was probably a lot of money to him. She'd gladly pay him that much to marry her and they would both walk away after six months. What could be simpler?

Instead, when he left her in the rain outside the cabin, she was no better off than when she made the three mile walk into town.

Nothing had changed. She still needed that money. Tonight, something was obviously bothering him. Maybe if she approached him when he wasn't trying to drink away his problems she'd get a different outcome.

Toweling herself dry, she put on a long t-shirt and shorts, crawled into bed, and spent most of the night tossing and turning. Occasionally she fell asleep only to wake when images of debt collectors and handcuffs bled into her dreams.

Bleary eyed but resolved, she got a ride into town first thing the next morning and sat on the stoop outside his apartment waiting for him to emerge. She wasn't brave enough to knock this time, but she hoped he wouldn't sleep all day because it was cold out here. The rain had stopped sometime after midnight and the temperature dropped twenty degrees. A milky sun glittered on the silver domed silos across the road but offered no warmth. According to the weather app on her phone, spitting snow was expected this afternoon. Growing up in the Florida panhandle, she'd heard that phrase before, but she'd never seen it.

How cold did it get at the forty-fourth parallel? The warmest things she owned were this funnel necked hoodie and slip-on sneakers which were already proving to be no match for the weather. If she had to sit out here much longer, she'd freeze to death.

Behind her, the apartment door opened. Prissy rose and swung around.

"What do you want now?" Logan Shaw groaned.

An improvement over last night's barking and cursing.

"I came to accept your offer."

He leaned against the doorframe, arms folded over his chest, eyebrows raised. "You want to get naked and have sex with me?"

If she wasn't so desperate, she'd slap his face for that. Instead, she remembered the money, and why she needed it, and managed a calm reply, "No. I want to pay you ten thousand dollars to marry me."

"Sixty."

"Excuse me?"

He closed the door and brushed past her.

"I said fifty percent." He spoke over his shoulder. "If you get twenty thousand when you marry and a hundred after six months, that means I get ten at the wedding and fifty with the divorce. Ten plus fifty equals sixty thousand."

"Wait a minute!"

He ignored her, of course.

She picked her way down the frosty wooden steps as quickly as possible, but with his longer strides he reached the bottom long before she did. She sprinted across the gravel yard to keep up with him.

He reached for the truck's door handle, but she threw herself against the panel in front of him as if her splayed arms would stop him from leaving. "I never said you'd get half the signing bonus *and* half the final check." Her vocal cords, already aggravated by the cold and the exercise of chasing after him, had tightened up until her voice was barely a whisper.

He shrugged like he could care less. Since she knew that was true, she wheezed more oxygen into her constricted airway and argued as forcefully as possible, "But I already agreed to five thousand more than my first offer."

"Sixty or no deal." He grasped her shoulders and moved her aside so he could open the truck door. Keys dangling from the fingers of his right hand, he slid onto the driver's seat and reached for the door handle with his left.

"Wait!" Inserting herself into the space between him and the door, she looked into his dispassionate face and realized there really was no choice but to surrender. It was painful. Aggravating. Humiliating. "Okay."

"Get in."

She had barely climbed into the passenger seat before he put the vehicle into gear. She pulled her door closed to avoid tumbling out onto the ground and by the time she buckled her seatbelt, they were already in town.

Did this mean he accepted her offer? Or was he driving her back to her cabin? She opened her mouth to ask, caught a glimpse of his angry profile, and kept quiet.

They reached the town common and the red covered bridge spanning the center. On her first day in Ammonoosuc Falls, the reality show contestants were photographed in front of that one hundred-and fifty-six-foot marvel of engineering. The film crew then doctored the photo to add a river beneath the bridge and change the sign to an imaginary location in Vermont.

Logan drove halfway around the common before turning down a side street.

Apart from that first day and a few planned and scripted outings, the reality show contestants rarely saw anything other than their lodgings and set locations, so she was unfamiliar with this part of town. "Where are we going?"

He ignored her question to ask one of his own. "What's your name?"

"Prissy."

"Bull."

"What's that supposed to mean?"

He braked for a stop sign at a four-way intersection and looked left and right. With no oncoming traffic, he continued straight into a large parking lot shared by an emergency services building, public library, and town hall.

When he had parked the truck he glanced at her as if she was a simpleton. "I mean, what is your *real* name? Not some silly thing you made up for the tv show."

"My name really *is* Prissy," she gritted, wanting to do bodily harm to someone for the first time in her life. She imagined pulling the hair out of his head one strand at a time. If only she didn't need that money.

"Your whole name?" he bit out.

"Priscilla Daphne Nicole Schermerhorn, but everyone calls me Prissy."

Doubt crossed his otherwise handsome features. On the set, he had charmed the cast and crew, but his amiable personality went into hiding whenever she was around. This, the suspicious, disagreeable Logan Shaw, seemed reserved just for her. "Show me your license."

She dug into her tiny crossbody bag and pulled out the Florida identification, reluctantly placing it in his outstretched palm. He stared at the card for a minute, at the image of her face and the printed details, then flipped it over to read the back.

Instead of returning it to her when he was done, he cupped it in his hand and shook his head while removing the keys from the ignition. "What were your parents thinking?"

"Hey!" She reached for her license, but he was already out of the vehicle. Hastily unbuckling her seat belt, she scrambled after him, catching up just as he cleared the concrete path to the town offices. "What are you doing?"

"Applying for a marriage license." He shook his head and held the door open for her to enter the building. She was shocked by the polite gesture. He seemed surprised as well, shaking his head again as she passed and muttering, "Damned if I know why."

Prissy didn't have a moment to absorb that decision, celebrate, or sigh in relief because when they entered the building his face changed completely. Gone was the surly, rude, insulting Logan Shaw. In his place a friendly stranger greeted the couple waiting in line ahead of them. Ignoring her as if she didn't exist, he asked about their children, who he obviously knew, and their plans for the upcoming Thanksgiving holiday.

The man was giving her whiplash.

The first customer finished her business and the couple stepped up to the service window. Beside her Logan relaxed, only to tense again when a tall redhaired man came in.

Groaning beneath his breath, he schooled his features into the usual, reserved-for-everyone-else, expression before greeting the newcomer. "What's up?"

Someone he knew well, then.

"Dropping off an invoice at the station," the man nodded his head toward the door and, she assumed, the fire department across the lot. "I saw your truck here. How are you holding up?"

Logan shrugged, swallowed, angled his body away from her. Whatever this was about, he clearly didn't want her knowing more.

The man clasped his shoulder. "Glad to see you didn't drink yourself stupid last night. Though no one could blame you if you did."

Logan nodded and, noticing her standing next to him for the first time, his friend changed the subject. "I thought you were all done with the film crew?"

"Yeah." Logan gave her a look that clearly said, 'Don't blow this or I'll back out of our deal.' To the other man he explained, "She needed a form. I gave her a ride into town since it's cold out and she was walking."

A plausible lie. Did his friend know him well enough to recognize it as one? Apparently not, because he grinned and said, "Always a sucker for the ladies."

"Don't I know it." Logan shifted his weight from one foot to the other. Was that a tell? "Speaking of ladies, is Ivy home today? Or at work?"

"She was going into the office for a few hours."

"Good, I've got some questions for her."

The man opened his mouth as if to say something else, glanced her way, and simply finished with, "She'll be glad to hear from you."

The couple at the clerk's window finished their transaction, and the redhead followed them out with a wave over his shoulder to Logan. "Later."

A vacuum of awkward silence filled the vestibule. He had deliberately not introduced her to the people in line ahead of them; deliberately not explained to his friend why she was here with him. Prissy didn't expect a real marriage, but could she look forward to six months of this?

"Can I help you?"

Then his behavior didn't matter, because he stepped up to the town clerk's window and said the words she needed to hear. "We came to apply for a marriage license."

It was almost anti-climactic. Five minutes after he made that announcement, they were in the truck again. "Where to now?" she asked. Not really expecting a reply, yet still mildly disappointed when she didn't get one.

He left the downtown area and drove south out of Ammonoosuc Falls. She noted the road signs like breadcrumbs in case he changed his mind and dumped her in the middle of nowhere to find her own way back.

After a few miles of driving, he pulled off the highway and parked in front of a metal industrial building backed by an open gravel pit. The sign out front identified the business as JLC Sand and Gravel.

"We're getting a prenup. If I say anything in here that doesn't sit well with you, walk away. I won't stop you. But listen closely; this is not a negotiation."

She slid out of the truck and followed, sticking her tongue out behind his back.

"I saw that."

Well, of course he had. The plate glass entry doors were as good as a mirror. Did she care? Not really.

He led her through an open office past three desks to a glass paneled room in the back corner. A nameplate on the desk inside identified the woman bent over the keyboard as Ivy Gordon, Attorney-at-Law. She looked up on hearing them enter.

"Hey, Logan. I wasn't expecting you today. How are you doing?"

"Yeah." He ignored her question and glared a warning at Prissy. "Ivy, this is Priscilla Schermerhorn. We're getting married and I don't want anyone to know about it, or about her. We need a prenup so when we divorce next year my assets are protected."

That wasn't the worst humiliation of the day. Oh, no, he followed with a whole menu of embarrassing and demeaning conditions for her.

"You agree to make no claims against any of my property, including the house."

That one was no problem.

"We'll split the money from the television show, fifty-fifty."

As much as it pained her to agree to that, she did.

"And you'll pay half our living expenses; heat, electricity, property taxes, insurance, cable television, and groceries."

"How am I supposed to do that on ten thousand dollars?" she demanded.

His answer was succinct. "Get a job."

He would file for divorce exactly six months from their wedding ceremony, citing irreconcilable differences, protecting his reputation and implying that she was to blame for their failed marriage. She didn't like that, but at least he wasn't filing for cause.

She would pay half the court costs. Not unexpected.

"If at any time this marriage is consummated," his frown made clear the unlikeliness of that ever happening, "you're responsible for birth control. And you won't have any relations with other men while we're married."

Her face turned beet red when he laid down that stipulation, and even the attorney's jaw dropped. That reaction was probably the only reason he tacked on, "And the same goes for me."

The last condition was a complete surprise. "I'll manage all your finances."

He started on that as soon as they were back in the truck. "Hand me your wallet."

Numb, she slipped the billfold from her crossbody bag and gave it to him.

"Pink." Disgust colored his voice as he handled the feminine leather purse. "Why am I not surprised?"

Reaching across her lap, he opened the glove compartment, and she shrank back against her seat the way a person might react to a venomous snake because it can dart suddenly, and strike without warning.

He grabbed a pair of scissors then emptied the contents of her wallet onto the truck console between them. Thirty dollars cash and a handful of coin, a debit card, credit card, passport, and two Red Cross certification cards spilled across the vinyl surface. He put the First Aid and Water Safety Instructor cards back into their slots and added her driver's license, which had still been in his possession. The loose change he threw into a cup on the console. The bills, passport, and debit card were returned to her wallet, but the credit card he kept. "From your parents?"

She nodded.

Holding it up so she could see what he intended, almost like a dare, he cut it into four small pieces before dropping two in the coin cup and putting the others in his back pocket; making it impossible for her to retrieve and read the account number.

"That's not fair," she objected, clearing her throat because even to her own ears it sounded like she was whining. "They gave that to me for emergencies."

"From now on you'll pay your own way." He returned the scissors to the glove compartment but didn't start the truck.

"Are we waiting for something?" she finally asked, after they had sat there for several minutes without any explanation from him.

"Witnesses."

Okay, so she'd have to drag the answer out of him. "Witnesses to what?"

"The marriage ceremony, of course."

"What? Now!?" At his nod, she protested. "But my family needs time to get here. And I don't have a dress! There are, like, a million things to plan."

"This isn't a wedding, sweetheart." The last word was a sneer. "It's a marriage. A business agreement, in case you weren't listening in there or forgot your own proposition. You're marrying me for money. You don't get a bouquet of flowers or a guest list. And the sooner we do this, the sooner I can file for divorce and be rid of you."

A car pulled into the lot and parked beside them.

"Let's go."

Chapter Three

Logan watched her sulking in the passenger seat. Cheek pressed against the window, shoulder rolled away from him, she clutched her crossbody bag in both hands as if she feared he'd take the rest of the contents away from her.

He almost laughed, remembering her shock when he cut up the credit card. He had half expected her to bail on this whole arrangement then, but she just sucked in a breath, doe brown eyes wide, and held her tongue. That was killing her, he could tell, because she was a yapper. Yet the less he had to listen to her wispy little voice, the better they would get along.

He had deliberately hurried her this morning. If he gave her time to think, to question what they were doing, she might back out and despite not needing her sixty thousand dollars, or even the first ten, he did need a wife.

Twenty-four hours ago, he was shoveling dirt into the grave of his only family member. Last night he was drinking away his sorrow. Then in the wee hours of this morning, he got a text from Dummer's girlfriend Cherilyn that changed his life and suddenly Super Ditz's proposal was more timely opportunity than insult.

Their vows were the bare minimum.

"Do you, Logan Shaw, know of any legal reason why you may not be joined in marriage to Priscilla Schermerhorn?"

"I do not."

Ivy asked the same question of his intended who replied in the same way.

"I, Logan Shaw, take you, Priscilla Schermerhorn, to be my wedded wife."

He thought she might choke when it was her turn to say wedded husband. Part of him wanted to laugh at the expression on her face. Her little nose wrinkled with distaste, but she swallowed back the words she probably wanted to say and repeated the vow.

Watching her screw up enough courage to go through with this farce, he noticed how thick her eyelashes were. A shade darker than the mass of caramel streaked blond hair falling like a waterfall to her waist. She had a little girl's body, small breasts and narrow hips, but her mouth was that of a porn star.

What the hell? She was a means to an end, nothing more. Yet he would give her his name and a place to live for the next six months if it meant honoring his brother's dying wish.

That thought cracked his heart wide open.

"Did you hear me?"

Ivy must have spoken to him.

"I said you may kiss your bride."

Not likely. A minute ago, he was cataloguing her features, admitting they weren't awful, but now he couldn't even look at her. Guilt, he realized, for thinking of anything but his brother.

So, he lifted his bride's ringless left hand and gave her knuckles the briefest possible salute. They signed the license where necessary, watched as the witnesses did the same, then he hustled her out of the building with the excuse that they wanted to make it to the town clerk's office before it got too busy.

The truth was he didn't want her getting friendly with Ivy. This was a temporary arrangement satisfying both their needs, and he didn't need her any more involved in his life than a roommate would be.

They filed their marriage certificate with the clerk, then met the reality show's producer at A Notch Above restaurant. Luckily none of the kitchen staff had arrived yet. The last thing he wanted to explain to his employees was why they were together, which would mean explaining to Prissy that he owned the place. She thought he was a simple security guard and for now, that's all she needed to know.

Just to be safe, he urged the producer to hurry through their paperwork, saying they had to get to the bank in Woodsville and deposit the check before they closed for the day.

"I don't know why you made such a big deal about having *and* between our names when they wrote the check," Super Ditz grumbled now from the passenger seat of the truck.

"If a-n-d is between our names, we both have to sign the back. This way you can't cash it without me knowing."

"I said I'd share, fifty-fifty. I don't lie."

Logan didn't bother replying. With few exceptions, the women in his life had all lied to or abandoned him. Trust was not something he gave away for free.

"Besides, you've got my word on that stupid prenuptial agreement."

Ignoring her again, he said, "When the check clears, we'll open a six-month CD for you. You have to practice the pay-yourself-first principle. Save ten percent of everything you make and don't touch it, starting with your half of the check."

"Why are you in charge of my money?"

Her voice was quieter now. Dispirited. He couldn't let himself care. She was the one who came to him, treating him like a gigolo available for a price, assuming he'd accept five thousand dollars for the privilege of spending six months with her.

"I'm in charge because you don't know how to manage it." Before she could object, he added, "If you did, you wouldn't be so desperate. You wouldn't have proposed to me last night."

She had no comeback for that and remained silent on the rest of the drive to Woodsville.

"Give me ten bucks," he said when they reached the bank.

"I only have thirty!"

"How much can you get with that debit card?"

Face flaming, she dug a ten dollar bill out of her wallet and handed it to him. He read her embarrassment to mean she'd emptied the account her card was linked to. All the more reason for him to manage her funds.

Inside the bank, they opened a joint account with her ten and another from him, plus the check from the show which would take a few days to clear. He made sure both signatures were required for any withdrawals from the account.

"What now?" she asked when they were back in the truck.

Instead of answering, he drove to a nearby department store and left her in the parking lot while he went inside to the sporting goods section.

Reality was setting in. His gut burned with a mixture of guilt, heartbreak, and anger. Guilt, because he took vows with a woman he didn't respect one day after burying his brother. Heartbreak, because he had waited ten years to move into his new house with Dummer, and now he would live there with her instead. Anger, because he was taking his pain out on her even though she didn't deserve it, yet he couldn't seem to stop.

He stomped through the department store. He yanked items off the shelves as if they had personally offended him. Knowing he was out of control and no fit company for anyone, he paid at the self-check-out register rather than subject an innocent clerk to his foul mood.

He returned to the vehicle with long strides meant to put space between himself and his feelings. Impossible.

When Super Ditz asked, "What's that?" he barely kept from biting her head off.

"Your wedding present."

Tossing the sleeping bag and camp pillow into her lap without looking at her, he started the engine and reversed out of the parking spot.

His stomach grumbled. One more complaint he could lay at her feet, because if not for her early morning visit, he would have had breakfast at the diner. And, more importantly, coffee.

Maybe she ate before coming into town, but by now she was probably just as hungry as he was. He should stop being a jerk and get her a sandwich. That would be the gentlemanly thing to do, but he didn't trust himself to talk right now. As bad as he had been to her last night, he wasn't sure he could even be that civil now.

So instead of feeding her, he drove to the cabin she had been living in and waited outside while she packed up her belongings. The rest of the Ditz Brigade came out with her when she was done, gushing and smiling at him as if this marriage proved fairy tales really do come true.

Killing their illusions, he stayed behind the wheel while Super Ditz hauled her luggage across the yard and heaved it up into the truck. She was little and it was bulky, maybe even half her weight, but if he put his hands on it he might chuck it into the Ammonoosuc River.

Once they were back at his apartment he said, "I have stuff to do," and was kind of proud of himself for not swearing. Or howling in pain. "The door's unlocked."

PRISSY DRAGGED HERSELF out of the truck beside the staircase, physically and emotionally exhausted from the events of the last twenty-four hours.

"Don't forget your stuff."

Dropping the sleeping bag and pillow at her feet, she returned to the cab and pulled out both suitcases. She had barely cleared the side panel before he sped away, gravel spraying up from the truck tires and pelting her shins through her tight leggings.

"How does it feel to get what you want?" she whispered to the empty yard. On the verge of crying because what seemed like such a great solution to her problems last night was turning into the biggest fiasco of her life.

She should be committed.

A humorless smile twisted her lips and dried the moisture in her eyes. She already was, wasn't she? Just not in the you're-too-crazy-to-trust-out-in-public way. Instead, she was sentenced to six months with a man who reserved foul language and rude behavior just for her.

Now she could either stand out in the cold with her luggage, feeling sorry for herself, or haul it up to his apartment and get the first day of that one hundred eighty-day sentence over with. She threaded her wrist through the sleeping bag straps, tucked the pillow beneath one arm, and grabbed her suitcases.

They banged against her ankles with each tread she climbed. The pillow kept slipping from her armpit to her hip before she caught it with her elbow. She had to stop and readjust the load three times before finally reaching the top of the stairs.

Last night, nerves kept her focused on her mission: Get Logan Shaw to marry her. Now, with that anxiety gone, she stepped inside and took her first real look at the place where he lived.

"Appalling." From the bare floor to the nude counters to the room empty of furniture but for a gaming chair in the corner, the place was hideous. Not a single rug, not a towel or refrigerator magnet in sight. The only curtain was the one beside the door, probably just to block people like her from looking in while they stood on the stoop.

Leaving her things on the floor where a welcome mat should be, she explored the rest of the apartment.

His bedroom consisted of a mattress on the floor without a box spring. A set of sheets, still in store packaging, sat in the middle of a puffy gray comforter and two bare pillows were stacked against the wall like a makeshift headboard. There was a closet with hangers but nothing on them. A shelf above the rod held folded stockings and underwear. Pants and shirts were stacked on the floor beneath. A pile of wrinkled clothes sat in the corner next to a box of garbage bags, presumably used for carrying dirty laundry out for washing.

One beer branded towel hung on a hook beside the shower in the adjoining bathroom. A combination shampoo and bodywash was the only thing inside that cubicle. Under the sink she found six face cloths and one electric razor. Above the sink was a single electric toothbrush and a tube of toothpaste. There was no trash can. No hand soap. No floor rug. Two rolls of toilet paper sat on the back of the commode; one was open.

"This will never do," she muttered. Homes were meant to be beautiful, comfortable places where one escaped the outside world. Not...this.

Yet she couldn't do anything about it, with two ten-dollar bills to her name and barely four times that left on her debit card.

Get a job, he had said. She would knock on every door in Ammonoosuc Falls until she found employment; right after she got something to eat.

His refrigerator held nothing but beer and a single stick of butter.

The Chiswick Diner served lunch, she knew, but it was at least a mile from Logan's apartment. She could either walk there or starve.

She chose to walk.

Arriving at the diner short of breath and with cold-numbed toes to find an empty parking lot almost made her laugh, wondering how her life had turned into this dark comedy.

Yet the restaurant lights were still on, and the door was unlocked, so she stepped inside hoping to get warm before trudging back to the empty four walls of Logan's apartment.

"Kitchen's closed," said a lone woman wiping down tables inside. "You can get something at Campbell's Country Store." Slinging the towel over her shoulder, she ran a forearm across her forehead, pushing auburn curls out of her eyes. "They serve a mean sandwich."

"Thank you." Prissy turned to go, but when the woman started flipping long benches upside down onto tables, she stepped forward to help.

"You looking for a job?"

"Yes." The last bench was in place, and Prissy had pulled the drawstring on her hoodie tight in preparation for going out into the elements, but the woman's question stopped her. "Are they hiring here?"

"I am." She stuck out her hand and Prissy took it, receiving a hard, brisk shake. "Shelly Twomey. I'm the owner. You have any experience in a diner?"

"Not a diner, no, but I have some restaurant experience." As a hostess at an all-inclusive summer resort during high school. The kind of place where families spent a week or two, played golf, and learned to swim. A far cry from a small-town eatery with printed menus and the general public for clientele, but Shelly didn't ask for details, so Prissy kept them to herself.

"One of my waitresses quit this week without notice. When can you start?"

Was getting a job in Ammonoosuc Falls really this easy? "I can be here tomorrow."

"You're hired."

Ten minutes later, Prissy had filled out the necessary paperwork. "Just a formality," Shelly said, which was good, because Prissy had to leave some things blank. She didn't know her current address. The film crew's post office box would remain open until the end of the year, so she listed that for mailing and River Road for her physical address. She used her maiden name because she wasn't sure if Logan ever planned to announce their relationship. He told Ivy it was a secret. He swore the witnesses and bank manager to secrecy, saying they planned to surprise her family with the news before telling everyone else, but that could take a few weeks.

Such a charming liar.

If she put Shaw on the form, would he accuse her of broadcasting their marriage? Pretty sure she knew the answer to that question, she wrote Schermerhorn on the line and handed the application over.

Shelly gave the form no more than a cursory glance. "Be here at six tomorrow. You'll shadow Terri for breakfast, Darla for lunch. We don't have official uniforms, but everyone wears white tops, black bottoms, no underwear on display, hair off your shoulders. Any questions?"

Yes, where to find appropriate clothing between now and then, but Prissy didn't ask. Instead, she thanked Shelly and made the trek back to town. Up and down a long hill, across a huge field against a powerful wind that sliced through her clothing and made her bones rattle. Her slip-on sneakers were no more protection against the bitter weather than her hoodie. By the time she reached the common her toes were numb, and her teeth were chattering.

Her stomach had stopped growling half a mile ago. When her hunger returned, it would be like a bear roaring to life after winter hibernation, but her clothing needs came first.

The town held two possible options: Kelly's What-Not Shop and the North Country Trading Post. Since the last one was closer, she started there.

The store carried a variety of outdoor equipment, but they also had Army/Navy surplus goods at ridiculously low prices. She left with two pairs of lightweight black tactical pants from the boys' section and clunky black combat boots guaranteed not to blister, at least not too much, with first use. Just to be safe, she grabbed three pair of thick men's socks for extra protection.

Shelly said everyone wore white shirts at the diner yet implied there wasn't a standard. Prissy added a package of men's white t-shirts to the stockings and found three vintage silk scarves at the What-Not Shop.

Her bank account now drained to pennies, she stepped out with her bags in hand and almost ducked back inside when a cold blast of moisture laden wind slapped her in the face.

Campbell's County Store was on the opposite side of the common. She took advantage of the covered bridge for both its shelter and the shortcut it offered to cross the green.

"Now this is my kind of place," she said on stepping inside the general store. Rustic, with an oiled wood floor, densely packed shelves, and a small dining section in the corner. Most importantly, it was heated. While reading the wall- mounted chalkboard menu, she stood over a floor vent and let the warm air flow resuscitate her frozen body.

"Can I get you anything?" the girl behind the counter asked after several minutes had passed with Prissy making no move to order.

"Thank you. Amy," she added, reading the girl's nametag. "I'd like a Croque Monsieur sandwich and hazelnut coffee."

"That will be fourteen ninety-nine."

Prissy handed over her last remaining ten-dollar bills and put a dollar of her change in the tip jar on the counter. She didn't feel a single qualm about it since she would be making money of her own tomorrow.

"Is this for here or to go?"

Any easy question. This place was warm. Furnished. And the angry new husband was somewhere else. "Here."

"What's the name?"

"Prissy."

Half an hour later she left with her body and spirit restored. She had a job. She had six months reprieve from worrying about tomorrow, or next week, or what she was going to do with the rest of her life. Best of all, she had a plan for climbing out of the financial hole she was in.

Chapter Four

One advantage to having Ivy Gordon on retainer for his business was that Logan could go to her for legal advice about his personal problems. After dumping Super Ditz off at the apartment, he returned to the Sand & Gravel office, unsurprised to find Ivy waiting for him.

"What is going on, Logan? Have you lost your mind?"

"No." He took a seat across the desk from her and spelled out the situation.

"Wow." She spun her chair from side to side, slowly, contemplating his dilemma. "And you're going to see Cherilyn's parents tonight?"

He nodded. "We're meeting at a restaurant in Dover. They don't know the real reason. I told them I had something for them from Dummer."

"I'd better come with you."

Logan was surprised by her offer. Relieved, too, yet he felt compelled to object. "I don't want to ruin your Saturday night plans."

She sprang to her feet and slapped her hands down on her desk blotter. "I'm in the mood for a good fight. Besides, you know darn well I have no social life."

"Then it's off to Dover we go."

The drive was just short of two and a half hours. Ivy was amazingly hyperactive for a bookworm and when she couldn't move, she gabbed. Her voice filled the truck's interior for the whole hundred and fifty minutes.

Logan tuned her out. Partly because he was used to her rambling monologues, the two of them being second cousins and having spent time together as children, and partly because he was too keyed up to manage a conversation.

When he finally pulled into the restaurant parking lot and turned off the ignition, his head ached. He uncurled his fists from the steering wheel and cracked his neck from side to side, rolling his shoulders free of tension.

"Good talking to you."

He gave Ivy a wry smile. "Sorry about that."

"No problem. Let's go rout this beast."

An hour later they sat in his truck, stunned into silence.

Logan held the keys in his hand but didn't put them in the ignition.

Ivy palmed her cell phone, flipping it over repeatedly, but she didn't use it.

Cherilyn's parents came out of the restaurant. Through the windshield, Logan tracked their movements from the front entrance to their car. Such an attractive, well-groomed couple. When he first met them, he envied Cherilyn for having two seemingly caring parents. He was happy for Dummer that they might be part of his future. Not anymore.

"God bless you," Ivy whispered. In her language that meant, 'better you than me.'

"They're bloodsuckers."

"An appropriate name for them."

Long after the leeches were gone, he finally started the truck, but they were on 101 heading west toward Manchester before Ivy broke the silence.

"You thought this might happen, didn't you?"

"Do you think they have a case?" he spoke at the same time.

"I think they're using what they do have to make you dance, and they're enjoying every minute of it. But your case is stronger."

"Even with my background?" His mother was a drunk and part-time prostitute, his father an unknown. He had spent time in courts as a child and the thought of appearing before a judge, even in chambers, even for a good reason, made his flesh crawl.

Yet at eighteen he had braved one for Dummer. The judge's words when denying him custody of his brother were etched in his memory. "While I commend your desire to take care of your brother, I don't think a man your age without work history or established credit can provide a stable home life for an eight-year-old boy."

To Logan's mind, anything was preferable to foster care. Yet he had swallowed that bitter disappointment and spent the next ten years preparing for the day they could be together.

Now here he was, alone, with another potential custody battle ahead.

"You definitely have the stronger case, as long as Cherilyn doesn't change her mind."

That's what worried him most. He was afraid their influence might be more powerful than her desire to honor Dummer's last wish.

"I had hoped we could work something out, you know," he admitted aloud.

"Hmm." Ivy was wise enough to keep her opinion to herself.

"Unfortunately, I need her cooperation, and she's a hormonal pregnant teenager who just lost the father of her child. Who is going to believe she knows what she wants?"

Ivy swiped her thumb across her phone screen. "I've got a friend who specializes in this area of law. Let me give her a call."

Logan half listened to her questions but paid more attention to her tone. Between Route 101 and Interstate 93, that went from inquiring, to attentive, to comprehending. After several versions of *uh-huh*, *okay*, and *I see*, she ended the call with a promise to stay in touch.

He was about to ask if she had any good news when she pre-empted him with a question of her own. "Are you going to tell me about your new wife?"

"What about her?"

"New Hampshire is a Closed Record state, but sooner or later people are going to find out you two got married. How long do you plan to keep it a secret?"

"Forever, if I'm lucky." A knee-jerk answer followed by a deep sigh. He lived in a small town by choice, and the chances of this news leaking were as good as snow falling in December.

"Okay, how's this. Why does she think you married her?"

"For the money."

"Which you can always use but don't really need. Will you tell her the real reason?"

"Not unless I have to. She could be my ace in the hole if this thing goes sideways."

"And you think she can play the part? Convince them you're a happily married couple?"

"She was on a reality tv show. Yeah, I think she can act."

They didn't speak again until they passed through the Hooksett toll booth. "You want to go straight home?" In a few miles he would have to take the exit to I-89 or stay on this highway. "Chris and I can bring your car over tomorrow if you want to leave it at the office."

"That sounds good. Prince must be worried about me by now."

Ivy rented a garage apartment from retired Dartmouth professors. While she worked, they took care of her Irish Setter, so he didn't have to be confined or sent to a kennel, but if she was gone too long, he'd start pacing and whining.

Logan moved into the right lane and exited onto the westbound route.

"Do you want to come in?" Ivy asked when they arrived at her home in Lyme.

"No, thanks. I'm beat."

"Okay." She opened the passenger door but didn't get out. "You'll have to tell her eventually."

"Tell who what?"

Ivy gave him that look she reserved for him, Chris, and Jamie. The one that made her look older than them instead of younger. Like a scolding nanny to a recalcitrant child, or a big sister to a baby brother.

"At least tell the guys."

"I will." They didn't share everything, but this was too big to keep secret, and he needed their support. "Thanks, and thanks for coming with me tonight. I don't know what I would have done without you there."

"Held your own," she said with absolute certainty.

He appreciated her vote of confidence. Yet over the next forty-five minutes he questioned almost every decision of his adult life. Giving up a full scholarship to the Tuck Business School at Dartmouth to provide a home for himself and Dummer. Instead, he had gone to the police academy so he could start working and saving, building the credit history the judge said he lacked. It hadn't mattered. When he tried again at twenty-two, a different judge handed down the same decision, this time using his unpredictable schedule as a reason for Dummer to stay in the foster home where he was already established. So, Logan earned a business degree around that schedule and started the sand and gravel business with Chris and Jamie. He worked weekends at A Notch Above then bought the restaurant with help from his friends when the owners retired.

His brothers from another mother.

How he hated that word.

The only woman who had ever loved him like a mother died when he was ten years old. Cora Dunlap Gordon; his great grandmother, and Ivy's grandmother.

The only one.

Shutting that train of thought down before it could suck him into a dark void of self-pity, he finally reached Ammonoosuc Falls and parked beside the staircase to his dark apartment. With any luck, Super Ditz had come to her senses and run all the way back to Florida.

Dragging his tired butt up the stairs., he didn't bother turning on any lights. All his furniture sat in a storage unit behind the sand and gravel building, except for the gaming chair in the corner and the mattress in the bedroom. His spatial memory was excellent. Six strides took him to the doorway between the main room and the bedroom, another three to the bathroom.

He stumbled on the eighth step.

"What the—?" Half bent and teetering in mid-air, he barely caught himself from toppling over by bracing one hand against the wall. With the other, he reached inside the bathroom and flipped on the overhead light.

Super Ditz. He should have known that instead of rolling her sleeping bag out in the living room, she'd put it here, directly in his path. She didn't even have the decency to wake up when he all but tripped over her.

Instead, she lay curled up like a human cocoon, blond hair barely visible above the top of the sleeping bag. He stepped over her prone form and closed the bathroom door behind him.

PRISSY WASN'T SURE what woke her. Blinking, she scanned her dark surroundings. Nothing but a formless void. Then she turned her head in the other direction and saw a sliver of light coming out from beneath the bathroom door.

She checked her phone where it was charging in a wall outlet. Ten-thirty.

"What was wrong with the other room?"

She squeaked and whipped her head around. "You scared me."

With his body backlit by the bathroom light, she couldn't see the expression on his face. Not that she needed to in order to read his mood. "Well?" That irritated tone was becoming all too familiar.

Then he leaned against the doorframe, arms folded over his chest, and the light kissed his handsome features. A shame such a rotten attitude was encased in such a pretty package. She mentally shook herself, remembering he had asked a question but not remembering what it was. "Excuse me?"

"Why aren't you sleeping in the other room instead of laying in the middle of this one?"

"I thought you might want to watch television without me being in the way."

That seemed to stump him. Like it hadn't occurred to him that she could be motivated by consideration rather than trying to complicate his life.

"Well, you might want to sleep closer to the wall."

"I roll."

"You what?"

"You know, during the night. I started out there, but I rolled away from the wall."

He flipped off the light. Apparently they were done talking.

Prissy punched her camp pillow and snuggled deeper into the sleeping bag. Obnoxious man. Gorgeous man. She needed to remember the first, but it was the second that followed her into her dreams.

Until her phone alarm went off at four thirty the next morning.

"What is *that*?"

Apparently he woke in the same foul mood he'd gone to bed in. "My alarm."

"Why is your alarm going off at this hour? It's dark out."

Yes, she was aware of that. Instead of responding, she unzipped her sleeping bag and went into the bathroom. She had already put her work clothes in the empty cabinet there, so she could get ready without waking him.

Once dressed, she rolled her sleeping bag up and slid the camp pillow between the straps, then stuffed both into the cabinet with the rest of her work clothes.

Back in the bedroom she navigated her way to his closet using light from her cellphone.

The air was chilly. Knowing it would be colder outside, she took a long-sleeved flannel shirt from his stack of clothing and put it on over her t-shirt then pulled on her hoodie.

The first thing she would buy when she had some money was a winter coat.

"What are you doing?"

There was no suspicion in his tone now, just curiosity.

"I got a job. I'm going to work."

"Huh."

That last was somewhere between an actual word and a mumble, like he had fallen asleep midway through speaking. Prissy tucked her phone in her pocket and strapped on her crossbody bag. Time to brave the elements.

On the top step she wanted to turn right back around. It was freezing!

Not just cold, but walk-in cooler cold, and so dark she couldn't see the stair treads. Hand gripping the railing, she picked her way down the steps by moving one foot at a time then waiting to make sure she wasn't going to fall before moving the other. Ice was new to her, but she'd noticed it could coat everything overnight and not melt until the sun rose.

That would probably be at least a couple of hours from now. In the meantime, she was grateful for the streetlight and the tread on her combat boots. The first let her stuff her hands in the pockets of her hoodie and not have to hold her cellphone out to see as she crossed the yard, the second kept her from falling more than once when she hit a patch of ice, and her feet almost went out from under her. Instead, she slid across the paved surface like a skater executing a half split before recovering.

Shelly said to be at the diner by six. Prissy arrived ten minutes early and was surprised to see the parking lot half full of vehicles. She hadn't realized they were open and serving already, but when she went inside the place was humming.

"Hi, table for one?" a middle-aged waitress asked.

"Terri, this is Prissy," Shelly interrupted, having just come out of the swinging doors between the kitchen and the counter. She carried a tray of glasses in her hands and talked while putting them away. "Get her an apron and an ordering tablet. She'll shadow you for breakfast, and Darla for lunch."

Eight hours later Prissy dragged herself out of the restaurant. Following someone around was exhausting. Her feet were numb. Her clothes smelled of food. Her hands were sticky from coffee, ketchup, and a dozen other food items despite washing them repeatedly.

She would have to trim her nails. Two broke during the breakfast shift but she had no clippers with her, so she tucked them into her palms rather than look sloppy before the customers.

They came from all walks of life. Loggers, truckers, a couple of state troopers and one local officer, two nurses Terri said worked the night shift at Dartmouth-Hitchcock and always stopped in on their way home, and the Sunday brunchers. The last were people who didn't normally go out, families and couples enjoying their weekend break, or folks just out of church.

"You're good with people," Darla observed after they waited on the first few tables.

"Thanks."

Yet the other waitress was territorial. "This will probably be the only day you shadow. Too bad. I think I'm getting better tips because they like you." She laughed but didn't offer to share any of those tips.

"No offense, but I'm not here to babysit. I'm here to make money. Shelly does the schedule on Sunday nights. This week you'll get your own hours and your own tables."

Terri had been willing to let her take some of her own, putting sixteen dollars in tips in her pocket. Yet Prissy spent most of the time observing, making coffee, clearing, wiping down, and resetting tables. She refilled condiment containers. She unloaded trays from the dishwasher. Plunged clear the backed-up toilet in the rest room. Mopped the floor when a toddler spilled a glass of juice.

They were allowed one meal if they worked a shift of five hours or more, but by the time she got to her poached egg on toast, it was cold, so she ate only the toast.

She left the diner wanting two things, food and a shower.

On the way back to the apartment she saw lights on at Campbell's Country Store. The warmth of the establishment beckoned. Conflicted, because she was hungry and cold but felt grungy and disheveled, she gave up the fight and stepped inside.

Heads turned when the bell above the door announced her arrival. Logan was one of the last to notice because he was leaning against the deli counter, smiling and talking with Amy. His expression turned into a scowl as soon as he saw Prissy.

Well, hello to you, too, she thought, advancing to the deli counter.

He straightened up, gaze wary. "What are you doing here?" His question was quiet enough that no one else would overhear.

"Getting lunch?" Or so she hoped, though Amy had walked away.

"You said you got a job. Where?"

"The Chiswick Diner."

"So, you have some tips?"

In reply, Prissy pulled the sixteen dollars from her pocket. He snatched it from her hand.

"Hey!"

He peeled off two ones and returned the rest to her. "Ten percent goes into savings." Folding the one-dollar bills in his gloved palm, he raised his voice to Amy who was replenishing a coffee urn in the center of the store, "I'll see you later, Amy. Have a good day!"

"You, too, Logan. Don't work too hard."

He didn't say goodbye to Prissy.

When she got back to the apartment with purchases she made in lieu of a deli sandwich; a can of tuna fish, a loaf of bread, a quart of milk, a jar of mayonnaise, and a jar of applesauce, she found a tin can on the counter with a note taped to it which read, "Ten Per Cent." Her two one-dollar bills were inside.

Chapter Five

The jar's contents grew as the temperature dropped.

Logan was out most nights, between the restaurant and working on the Dunlap place, but he was aware of winter coming on, and the meager contents of Super Ditz's wardrobe.

He'd also noticed the dark circles beneath her eyes.

The Chiswick Diner was busy. He'd seen the waitresses run themselves ragged trying to keep up with the number of customers who packed the place. The restaurant was also on the other side of town. If she was walking there, or even just walking back after her shift ended, that was a long trip in cold weather.

She'd have to have a coat. And a car.

"But I don't need one," she objected when he said something about it on their way to the bank in Woodsville the next day.

"You can't keep walking in this weather." He waved his hand at the windshield wipers beating out a tattoo across the screen in front of them, crusted with snow falling faster than they could manage.

"I only have ten thousand dollars! Well, nine after you took ten percent. How can I get a car with that?"

"What did you think? That you'd skate to work when we get freezing rain?"

"Freezing rain?"

He almost laughed at her parroting those words and the horror on her face. South Florida girl meets Mother Nature of the North, and what a nasty female she could be.

"I don't know how to drive in freezing rain," she admitted.

"If we get any, I'll drive you to work." Though he hoped that never happened. The less he heard of her wispy little voice, the better. "But you still need a car for the winter. What time do you leave in the mornings, anyway?"

"Five."

"You've got to be kidding me." Except when he helped Chris with plowing, he tried not to even blink his eyes open until six. "And when do you get home?"

"That depends when I get done. Usually around three."

Ten hours. He hadn't expected her to get a job this quickly, let alone one doing manual labor, and he admitted to himself that she had surprised him. But ten hours, on her feet? He glanced down at her black combat boots.

"Are your feet blistered?"

She grimaced. "I bought a box of bandages at the store."

Surprise mixed with sympathy. He wasn't drunk, his anger at her, and life in general, was now banked coals instead of raging flames. She had caught him on the worst day of his life last Friday. He still didn't like her, or any of the women desperate enough to sell themselves for six months, but he could have shown her more consideration than he had.

"We'd better add a shoe store and pharmacy to the list of places to go."

"I have shoes!"

"You should get some walking shoes for your job, at least."

"I'm not spending more money on shoes. The blisters will heal, and I'll get used to working in the boots."

She wouldn't budge on that. Or on buying a vehicle. At the used car dealership, they found a make and model he felt was reasonably priced but would require financing. She flat out refused. When he asked the salesperson to give them a moment, she hissed in her little girl voice, "I am not spending twenty thousand dollars on a car!"

"How much did you think you'd be spending?"

"A few thousand? I don't know, I've never bought one before, but it would be ridiculous for me to spend that kind of money for six months. Wait, make that six months minus seven days, since we've been mar—"

He clapped his hand over her mouth to prevent her from finishing that sentence.

She jerked her head out of his hold. "Anyway, it's a waste of money. I won't need a four-wheel drive, or all-wheel drive or whatever it is, in the Panhandle."

No matter how much he tried to reason with her, she wouldn't give. Even when he took her to another dealership across the river in Vermont, she complained that the prices were too high for her budget and the time she would be here.

That meant the shoe store was a waste of time, the car dealership the same. He was beginning to suspect she might be more frugal than he had first thought, but she ruined that assessment when they passed a florist shop.

"Oh! We need to stop for flowers."

"What? No."

"Yes. We need something for that apartment. I can put them on the kitchen counter or on the back of the toilet, but I'm tired of staring at blank walls."

"We are not getting flowers."

"It's my money."

"You haven't even bought groceries yet. And don't forget you're paying half the bills."

"And we need furniture," she continued as if he hadn't spoken. "I don't even have a chair to sit on."

"I have furniture."

"Oh, really?" She made a show of looking behind and around her. "Where is it hiding?"

Frustrated, Logan pulled into the shopping plaza. "It's in storage until the house is ready.

When we move in, I'll unload my stuff. I also plan to get some more from a furniture store, because the house has more rooms than the apartment."

"And when is all this happening?"

"Next weekend if everything goes well."

"You already bought the house?"

Thinking quickly, he said, "We'd already done the title search and survey before the reality show started. The owner just changed their mind about the price, so I couldn't sign for it until I had a bigger down payment."

She didn't question that explanation, but said, "Take me to see it."

"Not until next weekend."

"I won't know what to buy for my room."

"C'mon, get out of the truck. There's a bank branch here in the plaza where you can deposit your money, then you've got some shopping to do."

"We're not done talking about this," she said, though she got out of the truck.

"Yes, we are." He stepped down, shut the door, and started across the lot to the bank.

"You're going to show the house to me."

Logan stopped walking and she ran into him. When she stepped back, he said, "Listen, I'm doing you a favor today because you need stuff for your job, and I don't want you paying high prices for groceries at the general store. I'll need your money for bills," he added, just in case she thought he was doing any of this for her.

"But I won't be at your beck and call. You will buy a car so you can get yourself from point A to point B and not inconvenience me. And you are an inconvenience. I've got work to do, but instead I've wasted half an hour at the shoe store and an hour and a half at car dealerships."

"That was—"

He didn't let her finish. "Time I could have spent working. Not to mention the driving time." They were now in West Lebanon because there were a lot more shops and choices here than in Woodsville, but it was even further from Ammonoosuc Falls.

"That's not my fault."

He wanted to shake the argumentative woman. Girl. Woman-child. He didn't know exactly how to think of her, because she spoke like a little girl and with that elfin face and big brown eyes, she had a childlike quality. According to her license she was twenty-four years old. Right now, she was behaving like a petulant child half that age.

"You're the one who wasted our time," he said.

"I told you I wouldn't buy the shoes. You're the one who insisted we go there. I will buy a car, but not at those prices."

Logan turned on his heel and continued across the parking lot.

He heard her behind him, hurrying to catch up.

They mostly got through the rest of the shopping trip without an argument. She put a lamp in her basket, and he put it back. She passed the bath towels, and he grabbed one for her. When she spent way too much time inspecting grapes, debating between green or red, he solved the problem by grabbing a bag of each.

"Don't spend my money for me," she said.

"I'll pay for the second bag."

"No, you won't."

"I will."

He won that argument. Mostly, he thought, because she didn't want to have a dispute in front of other customers. He'd already figured out that while she didn't mind letting people know they were together—something he wanted to avoid—she didn't like having a public confrontation.

Something he remembered the next day when Chris and Jamie announced they were all going to the Chiswick Diner for lunch.

Jamie's wife Lauren was craving French fries, and since that was the only place in town to get them at this hour, he ended up sitting in a booth with the three of them and baby Emmy, hoping the flirty brunette would be their waitress.

No such luck. She delivered their water and said Prissy would be right with them.

"Isn't that one of the ditzes?" Chris asked. "There can't be two women with that name."

Logan didn't get a chance to answer, because Prissy finished at a table in the corner and approached their booth, the welcoming smile on her face faltering briefly when she saw him but probably not enough for anyone else to notice.

"Hello, I'm Prissy. I'll be your waitress today. Can I start you off with something to drink?"

Relief made him sag against the banquet seating because she was acting like she didn't know him. They ordered beverages and as soon as she turned her back, Chris said, "It's the ditzy girl from the cabin. My sister Sarah said she has more air upstairs than the rest of the airheads."

Logan was annoyed. First, that she had probably overheard some of what Chris said and even though he himself thought of her in those terms, he wouldn't say it aloud in a public place. Second, he wasn't sure if that assessment was entirely true. He still hadn't figured her out.

She returned with a tray of drinks and put them on their table wearing the same smile. Maybe she hadn't heard Chris after all. "Are y'all ready to order?"

"My wife is first," Jamie chuckled. "She's pregnant and desperate for some greasy fries."

"Stuff can't be good for the kid," Chris observed.

"I expect depriving a pregnant woman of her cravings can't be good for anyone in the vicinity," Prissy said with a wink for Lauren. "You want something to go with those fries?"

She was laying on the charm, Logan noticed, and not just with their table but with all the diners. Her service was fast. Her manner was sweet. And somehow she made the white t-shirt and black cargo pants look stylish. Her hair was up in a messy bun, a floral scarf wrapped around her shoulders like a shawl and twisted into a knot at the side of her neck. She had simple gold hoops in her ears and a slim gold watch on her wrist. Emmy pointed to it and said, "Pretty."

"Here." Prissy slipped the watch from her wrist and handed it to the toddler.

"Oh, no," Lauren objected, intercepting the exchange. "She'll drool all over it."

"It can be washed."

"The parts are too small," Logan said. "She might choke on them."

"Oh." Flushing, Prissy took the watch back and strapped it to her wrist. "I'm sorry."

"It's fine. We've got some toys in her diaper bag, anyway," Lauren said, "but thank you."

Prissy left with their order and Logan found himself facing two pair of censuring eyes. Lauren's gaze held surprise, Jamie's was questioning, but neither one were pleased with him.

"What's going on?" Chris asked. He had been reading a message on his phone, now he looked between the three of them. "What'd I miss?"

Jamie answered. "Logan being a di—"

"Jerk," Lauren corrected, with a side glance at their daughter.

"A jerk to the waitress."

"I wonder why she's still here?" Chris mused. "The other ditzes left last weekend. Cabin's empty."

"She was at the town hall when I saw you there Saturday," Jamie remembered, eyeing Logan. "You said she needed a form. Any idea what she was up to?"

Logan shook his head, taking a big gulp of coffee so he wouldn't have to speak.

The conversation turned to other things, and the subject was dropped until Prissy returned to collect their empty plates. She was stacking them on her tray when Chris spoke. "Weren't you supposed to leave town already?"

He wasn't being rude. Not intentionally, anyway, but he sometimes missed social cues, and this was one of those times. Because anyone could see Prissy stiffen up at the personal question. Yet she answered politely. "I'm sticking around for a while."

"How long?" Still not getting it. Or maybe he was interested in her?

"I'll be here for another six months."

Across the table Jamie raised his eyebrows and looked directly at Logan. Suspicion took root in his friend's mind and showed on his face. He knew the contract for marriage was six months if the contestants wanted a payout at the end. Logan and Prissy had both been at the town offices on Saturday. Jamie was putting two and two together and coming to the right conclusion.

Logan had to stop him before he got started.

"I've got to run up to Lisbon and meet with the road agent." He pulled his wallet from his back pocket and tossed a couple of bills on the table to pay for their meal. "You guys need anything?"

Chris shook his head. Jamie didn't speak, still giving him the squinty eye.

Lauren came to his rescue. "Say bye to Uncle Logan."

He peppered Emmy's cheek with kisses and gave her mother a single peck. "Later."

He was making the return trip south to Ammonoosuc Falls when the snow began. Big, fat flakes. Pretty. Heavy. Wet. Round two of yesterday's storm, which reminded him of their shopping trip to West Lebanon, which reminded him of the woman who slept four feet from his mattress in a military grade sleeping bag.

He couldn't think of her as Super Ditz anymore because he wasn't sure the title fit. He also couldn't think of her as Prissy because it was a silly name.

Whatever he called her, she would be getting out of work sometime in the next half hour and this wasn't a good day for walking. The snow would slow her down, but the real danger would be drivers on the road. Visibility was poor. The snow was slick. She could get hit by someone going into a slide or simply unable to see her before it was too late.

Aggravated by how quickly she was disrupting his life, he pulled over and sent Jamie a quick text rather than call and deal with questions, then drove to the diner.

PRISSY WISHED LOGAN and his friends hadn't come in for lunch. It was awkward waiting on them because she didn't know what her role in his life was supposed to be. Tenant? Roommate? Eventually people would realize they lived in the same place, and they'd need an explanation. Maybe she could ask him about it tonight.

In the meantime, she had to deal with the other wait staff drooling over him.

Darla was first. "O-M-G, I can't believe you got to wait on those three. If I'd seen them before they sat down, I would've made sure they went to one of my tables."

Prissy didn't point out that the restaurant had a seat yourself policy.

"They're all F-I-N-E fiiine," Darla drew out the vowel in the middle of the word and licked her lips. Three of them were sitting at a table counting their tips while the last table finished eating. "Of course, Jamie's off the market now, but I'd take either one of the other two."

"I like Chris best," Thalia said in a dreamy voice. "He's a big ox. You know what they say about big hands, right?"

The two of them giggled while Prissy's cheeks grew warm. She wasn't a prude, but she found nothing about Chris Cote attractive. He had been rude to her from the moment she moved into the cabin with the other contestants.

"That's okay," Darla said as if making a concession. "You can have him if I get Logan."

"Deal."

"Spill the tea, Prissy. Did they flirt? Leave a big tip? Ogle your pert little breasts?"

Prissy automatically looked down at her chest to make sure her scarf hadn't gone askew and revealed more than she wanted to.

Thalia laughed at her reaction. "She's just jealous because you can pull off an outfit like that. Her breasts would probably look like melons in a t-shirt."

Trying to put an end to their speculation, Prissy answered, "They didn't say anything." Rather, what they did say wasn't friendly. Logan scolded her for offering her watch to the baby and Chris asked questions that were none of his business.

"Too bad. I guess now that they're rich, they don't have as much time for girls like us."

"Rich?" Prissy thought of the barren apartment she slept in, and the hours Logan spent working security for the tv show.

"Not exactly," Thalia clarified. "But they're very successful, and if you look at their net worth it's probably in the millions now. Cash is another story."

"How do you know?"

"Because, Darla, I'm studying business at the Tech." To Prissy she added, "That's the community college in Berlin." Turning back to

Darla, she said, "So I know the difference between cash flow and net worth. They have property, and contracts, but I doubt they're flush with cash."

"I heard Logan's buying the Dunlap place."

"Yeah, I heard that, too."

"He has to have some money if he's getting that place."

"Hmm. I heard he bought it for Dummer and his girlfriend. That means he won't be asking you out." Thalia laughed, more of a spiteful cackle than friendly ribbing. She recorded her tips on the calendar for Shelly, then stood and pocketed them before grabbing her coat from the peg behind the booth they were at. "I'm out of here. You two have a good night."

Darla wrote her own tips down, cursing the other waitress under her breath.

Prissy didn't know what to say, so she kept quiet.

"She thinks she's so much better than me because she's going to college," Darla said. "But Logan was checking me out when I delivered their water." She almost preened with that announcement. "I'll show her."

Prissy kept her gaze on the calendar, watching while Darla recorded about two-thirds of the tips she actually made in the date square, then passed it across the table to Prissy.

"That snow is really coming down. Good thing my car has a remote start." She shrugged into her coat and pulled on her mittens. "I don't envy you walking in this stuff."

Nor did she offer her a ride.

Prissy would never let someone walk in this weather if she could help them, but again she kept quiet. She already had Darla figured out, and it wouldn't do any good to point out her thoughtlessness. Instead, she said goodbye, took the calendar into the kitchen for Shelly, and gave the dishwasher a hand mopping the floor so he could get out before the storm got any worse.

"I heard her." The teenager tilted his head toward the dining area where she had been counting her tips with the other waitresses. "I'd give you a ride if I had my car. My brother is putting snow tires on it today."

"Thanks, Ricky." She dumped the mop bucket out in the service sink and put it next to the one he had used. "That's very sweet of you."

He looked out the window of the kitchen door. "My ride's here."

"We'd better lock up, then."

They turned off the lights, double checked the front door, then went out through the kitchen into the falling snow. A familiar truck was parked at the back of the lot with its running lights on.

"Want me to ask my uncle if he can give you a ride?"

"No." The word came out of her mouth like a bullet. *Uncle*?

"Oh, okay." He seemed surprised by her vehement reply, and why wouldn't he be?

"Sorry, I don't want to put him out in this weather but thank you."

"Okay." He seemed to accept her explanation at face value. "Well, I'll see you later."

Chapter Six

Later turned out to be about two minutes after they parted. Prissy was on the road heading toward town when Logan's truck pulled up beside her with the passenger window rolled down. Ricky grinned, Logan leaned forward to look around him and speared her with a don't-argue-with-me-look. "Get in."

Not, 'may I offer you a ride?' or, 'can I give you a lift?' She decided to make him squirm a little for being such a boor. "I don't want to inconvenience you."

"He won't take no for an answer," Ricky warned.

"But you live in a different direction. Your uncle would be going out of his way." She added a sweet smile to those words, aimed squarely at Logan.

His jaw worked. He glanced at Ricky, back at her, and she could see the intent on his face before he opened the truck door and stepped down. He rounded the hood, pulled open the passenger side door, and said, "Get in before the snow gets any worse. Please."

That last word was just for Ricky's benefit. The teenager had already hopped out of the truck so she could have the middle.

Refusing would be churlish. Besides, the truck's interior looked much warmer than where she was standing, so she grabbed the door handle and climbed inside.

"Where to?" Ricky asked when all three of them were in the cab.

"I'll take you home first," Logan said, knowing it was a mistake even as he said it. Prissy being in his truck, even if Ricky said it was his idea—which Logan made him think it was—would be one coincidence too many for Jamie.

Proven the next morning when Logan showed up at the sand and gravel building. Chris and Jamie were leaning against their respective desks while Ivy had the interior shades drawn in her office. Hiding, which meant she knew what they were after but would hold her tongue because of attorney-client privilege.

He should have taken her well-intentioned advice and told them what was going on before it came to this.

"What's up with you and that reality show contestant?" Jamie asked before Logan had his coat off. "You want to fill us in?"

"No."

Jamie remained where he was, arms crossed over his chest. Of the three of them, he was the most grounded, most content, and that also made him the most patient.

Logan threw himself into the chair behind his desk and let out an exasperated sigh. In case they didn't already know he was reluctant to explain himself.

"She came to see me last week and asked me to marry her for five thousand dollars."

"What?"

"No way!"

Slightly mollified by their stunned reactions, Logan nodded. "She said she knew I wanted to buy a house and heard I needed money. If she married a local, even someone who wasn't part of the cast, the show would give her a twenty thousand dollar signing bonus and a hundred more after living with the guy for six months. She figured since I don't like her, I was a good candidate because we could both walk away after six months without any hard feelings."

"She's got some nerve," Chris whistled. "I mean, I knew she was ditzy, but this is something else. Did she really think you'd be stupid enough to take her on for six months?"

Jamie was more observant than the other man. Slowly, he unfolded his arms and stood in front of the desk he rarely used. He had a full-time automotive business and was more or less a silent partner in the sand and gravel corporation now.

Logan eyed him warily.

"You did it."

"Did what?" Chris' head swiveled back and forth between the two of them.

"He married her."

"What? No, he didn't."

"He's not denying it."

Logan now had their undivided attention. Jamie looked none too happy while Chris' mouth hung open in disbelief.

"I told her I get fifty percent or no deal."

"And she took the deal."

"She doesn't get anything else when our six months is up. I had her sign a prenup."

Chris glared at the blinds shielding Ivy from view.

"Don't blame her," Logan said, "you know she can't say anything as my attorney."

"She's the company attorney," Chris bit out.

"She's a private attorney who happens to rent office space from us. That means her clients are not our business, and when I'm her client, what we talk about stays between us."

"Let's get back to the subject at hand," Jamie interjected. "I do have to work today. Are you telling me this woman is living with you?"

Logan nodded.

"In your *empty* apartment? Is there even any furniture left there, or is it all out back?"

That question rankled, because it made Logan feel guilty about the barren apartment he left her in, which in turn made him angry. "You know I'm moving into the house next weekend." He hadn't known he'd be sharing space with a stranger when he put his stuff into storage.

Since the wedding, he had spent every night working on the place, before the restaurant opened and after it closed. Her breathing kept him up. Her alarm woke him when stars were still hanging in the sky. All of which meant he was beat and not in the mood for this interrogation.

"Then what?" Chris' question brought him back to their conversation. "Is she moving into the house with you?"

Logan nodded.

"The house you bought for Dummer?"

Tensing at the question, Logan inhaled a deep breath and forced himself, again, to let go of that dream. "Yeah, well he's not going to need it now."

That silenced his friends. They knew how hard he had worked over the last ten years to give his brother a permanent home.

"Sorry, man," Chris finally said.

"Yeah," Jamie agreed, "but that doesn't explain this wedding."

Logan took the telephone receiver on his desk off the hook so anyone calling the business line would get a busy signal. Jamie raised his eyebrows at the move.

"Cherilyn is pregnant with Dummer's child."

Chris' jaw dropped again. Jamie's head snapped back like he'd been punched. Their reactions mirrored his own when he first heard the news; before the rest of it came out.

"She's only seventeen. She doesn't want to raise a baby."

Silence met his announcement. A total, can't-hear-a-pin-drop kind of silence.

Logan didn't have to tell them how much that gutted him. He had been rejected and abandoned as a child. To have his niece or nephew rejected made his heart bleed, even though he understood where she was coming from.

"What are you going to do?" Jamie finally asked.

"I'm going to get the baby when it's born. I met with her parents this weekend to work out the details. Ivy went with me to confirm I was buying the house and would be able to provide a permanent home for it."

"What, *they* wanted the baby?" Chris looked appalled. Logan couldn't blame him. Cherilyn's parents hadn't done the greatest job raising her and her delinquent brother despite giving the appearance of good middle-class parents.

"They wanted her to put the baby up for private adoption."

Chris whistled long and low. "There ain't no coming back from that."

Truer words were never spoken. They had met with an adoption agency, then forbade her from contacting Logan, all while she was dealing with Dummer's illness, then grieving his death.

Monsters.

"Ivy got a court order preventing that. Now her parents will make me jump through hoops, prove I'm capable of taking care of a baby."

"Don't biological parents have the right to say?" Chris asked. "I mean, wouldn't the court automatically give it to you if that's what she wants?"

Logan shrugged. That was normally the case, but his experiences in court to date had taught him not to count on anything where the law was concerned.

Jamie grabbed the nape of his neck and shook his head. "She's your backup plan. The contestant," he clarified, "in case they decide you're not a real family man."

Logan put the phone receiver back on its cradle. "Exactly."

Chris nodded a couple of times. "That makes sense. I couldn't picture you wanting her for anything else. I mean, she's easy enough on the eyes, but—" he trailed off, shrugging—"you can have your pick of pretty women."

"Trust me. This is not a permanent arrangement."

"YOU HEARD ME, RIGHT?"

Prissy turned her face away from the passenger side window where she had been watching with fascination as her breath fogged up the glass. To a girl from the Florida panhandle, that was a unique experience.

"What did you say?"

Logan was driving her to work again, the third morning in a row. They hadn't had any snow since Thursday, and she walked home each day, but he insisted it was too dark at five o'clock to be safe.

"I said," he bit out between his teeth, irritated with her as usual, "that this is not going to be a permanent thing."

"Right. I put an index card up on the bulletin board at the diner."

He shook his head, exasperation plain on his handsome face. She wondered what it would feel like to ever be the recipient of a smile or even a neutral expression coming from him.

"And what did you write on this card?"

"I said I need a car for five thousand or less that will pass inspection and get me through the winter."

He pulled into the diner parking lot and drove around back to the kitchen door. "I'll find a car for you."

"You don't have to." Really, she didn't want him to. For one thing, she didn't want to put him out because everything about her seemed to annoy him. On Thursday night he came home with a stuffed armchair and a side table for her to use, but when she tried to thank him for it, he reacted like an alligator with its tail caught in a trap. She didn't want to owe him for anything else. Besides, she wanted to prove, to both of them, that she could take care of herself.

"Get out of the truck."

That phrase was becoming depressingly familiar. It was his way of ending a conversation with her. Instead of goodbye, or have a nice day, or any of the things even a complete stranger would say, he pretty much booted her out of the vehicle and took off before anyone could see who had given her a ride.

And just as she did every morning, she unbuckled her seat belt, opened her door, and said, "Thank you for the ride," before sliding to the ground and shutting the door behind her. Good manners were a hard habit to break.

Today was different from the other days, though. This time Darla was working the opening shift and she had been looking out the window when Logan drove in. As soon as Prissy cleared the back door, the other waitress pounced.

"What are you doing with Logan Shaw?"

Prissy unzipped her hoodie and hung it on the coat rack. "He just gave me a ride."

"How do you know him?" she asked, more suspicious now.

"I don't." Not exactly a lie. She knew very little about him, and he guarded his privacy like it was gold.

"So, he, what? Just saw you walking to work and offered you a lift?"

"More or less." Again, not exactly a lie. Prissy didn't like half-truths, to her they were the same as untruths, but Logan didn't want people to know they were married, and she had agreed to his terms.

"Maybe I should start walking to work," Darla said with an arch of her dark brows, but she finally walked away, and Prissy finished taking off her winter wear. She had tied an apron on and slipped an electronic order pad into her pocket when Ricky stuck his head around the doorframe separating the tiny room she was in from the kitchen.

"Don't let her bother you," he said.

Prissy liked the teenager. A lot. His hazel eyes beneath a swath of strawberry blond curls were filled with good humor and his laid-back manner hid the fact that he worked hard as the dishwasher. She had learned that Logan's friend Jamie was Ricky's half-brother. Jamie had raised Ricky and their younger brother Matthew since the boys were little because their mother was unfit to do so. When she died, they moved in with him. They referred to Logan and Chris as uncles, though technically they weren't related.

"She doesn't bother me," Prissy reassured Ricky now. Mostly because she'd be gone in six months. Otherwise, she'd have to confront the waitress for her petty behavior.

A few minutes later the diner opened, and she didn't have time to think about Darla's obsession with her husband and every other available man between the ages of eighteen and forty. She was so busy some of the barely healed blisters on her feet re-opened, but her apron pockets quickly filled up with cash.

"Things will slow down soon," Shelly warned when Prissy was counting her tips at a booth later that afternoon. "Deer season goes for another couple of weeks, so we'll get hunters, and the snowmobile crowd, but between Thanksgiving and Christmas there's always a lull."

Prissy recorded her tips on the calendar and passed it to Shelly.

The bell over the door jingled.

"I am *not* waiting on him," Darla hissed, sliding onto the bench opposite Prissy where she couldn't be seen by the tall, stooped gentleman who had just come in.

"He's probably here for coffee," Shelly said without reprimanding her employee. Prissy noticed her boss was way too easy on the staff and often let them talk back to her or say things that weren't appropriate. She looked exhausted yet told Darla, "Go home. I'll take care of him."

"I'll do it."

Prissy didn't give either of them an opportunity to respond, already out of the booth and on her feet. "Good afternoon, sir. I'm afraid the kitchen is closed, but I can offer you coffee and dessert if you're interested?"

The man's frail smile took years off his craggy face. "Thank you. I would love a piece of chocolate cream pie."

"Sure thing. You just take a seat and I'll be right out with it."

ON MONDAY HE ORDERED banana cream pie and introduced himself as Gil Peringer. They chatted for a few minutes about desserts, and the weather, and he left a twenty-dollar bill just as he had the previous day, which meant half the money was for his food and half was a tip for her.

Tuesday afternoon he arrived a little earlier than he had the previous two days. This time he ordered apple pie and asked Prissy how a girl with her southern accent ended up in northern New Hampshire.

"It's a little embarrassing," she admitted.

"Please," he waved to the bench seat opposite his own. "Are you allowed to sit and tell me your story?"

The dining room was empty of all but the two of them. "Just for a few minutes," she cautioned, sliding onto the bench. She didn't want to keep Ricky any later than necessary.

"You heard about that reality matchmaking show they filmed here?"

His rheumy blue-gray eyes widened. "You were in it?"

"Yes." Prissy's cheeks warmed. She was embarrassed by the desperate circumstances that put her there. Yet in six months less ten days—she was still counting down on the calendar—she'd be much better off than she was when she auditioned for that show. As long as she could make it to that half year anniversary without killing her surly husband.

"I liked the area," she told Gil now, thinking she was getting way too comfortable with half-truths, "so I decided to stay for the winter and see if it suits me."

"If you can survive January and February, you'll be home free."

"That's what I thought."

He must have caught something in her tone. "But you miss home?"

Not exactly. She'd been away almost six years now, between college and graduate school. Her older sister lived and worked in Miami; her little sister was at college. Home wasn't what it had been when she first left, and never would be again, but she wished the path leading back to it wasn't so difficult.

"I miss my family. But the heat there can be oppressive, especially in the summer."

"Hmmm."

"And I miss the flowers." She shrugged. "It might seem silly, but I'm used to things blooming all year-round and I miss the color."

"I like flowers myself," he admitted.

The kitchen door swung open, and Ricky poked his head around the panel, then seeing them, retreated back into the kitchen.

Gil slid his empty plate to the edge of the table and pulled out his wallet. "Are you working again tomorrow?"

"No, but I'll be here on Thanksgiving." Prissy accepted the twenty-dollar bill he gave her and collected his dirty dishes. "Do you want change?"

He waved her question aside. "You keep it. And I'll see you on Thursday."

On the walk home, Prissy congratulated herself for making a friend. Darla thought Gil was weird, Shelly thought he was lonely, and while conceding he might be a little of both, Prissy liked the man. She even liked Logan when he forgot to dislike her.

Each morning she got up before him and used the bathroom. When she came out, completely dressed, she rolled up her sleeping bag and pillow and stored them in the cabinet before going into the main room so she would be out of his way when it was his turn.

Sharing the apartment with him was a lot like two planets on separate orbit paths in the same solar system. Each one was aware of the other yet trying not to collide.

He grumbled his way through the first half hour of every day. Some of what he said carried over the sound of running water, mostly muttering and cursing about a stray blond hair in the shower or bumping his shin on her basket of toiletries on the shelf below the sink. Or how no one in their right mind got up that early.

She didn't point out that five o'clock wouldn't seem so early if he got in at a decent hour. Yet he returned late every night, woke her when he used the bathroom, then fell onto his mattress without saying a word.

Despite the grumbling and the avoidance, he still drove her to work. He gave her a chair and side table. He surprised her with a bag of grapes in the fridge and, just in case she doubted they were for her, left a note saying, *Eat them.*

She laughed at the command. Someone else might have written, *These are for you*, or *Help yourself*, but he was working hard at not liking her and this was part of that mission.

Chapter Seven

They managed to live as mostly polite strangers. That changed on Wednesday.

Blinking awake to barely gray light coming in through the bedroom window, Prissy stretched in her sleeping bag and wondered if she would ever need an alarm clock again. She reached for her phone to see what time it was. Four forty-eight.

A little dot on the screen told her she had a missed call from her older sister. She could go to the other room and listen to the message, but getting up might wake Logan, so instead she wormed her way deeper into the sleeping bag and pressed play.

"You're in trouble, Priss. Mom and Dad got your text that you wouldn't be home for Thanksgiving break, and they sent a care package to your dorm. When it was returned, they called the school and asked why they hadn't just forwarded it to you if you had moved to another building. I found out where you are with a quick Internet search. Are you crazy? If reality shows aren't stupid and desperate enough, you end up all over the Internet. And if I can find you, Mom and Dad can. Figured I'd better warn you before this thing blows up."

Prissy gripped the phone and stared at the now blank screen, her mind just as empty.

"Better come out of there before you suffocate."

Praying all Logan caught was muted noise, she folded her sleeping bag down and peeked out over the top.

"When were you going to tell your family that you dropped out of college?"

Of course, he heard it all.

"Couldn't cut it?"

Prissy shrugged. If only it was that simple.

"Maybe you were hoping the show would launch your career as a celebrity so you could just look pretty and do nothing?"

She barely heard his accusations. Panic was setting in, her mind replaying the message from her sister and running through the conversation to come with her parents. She always knew it would happen, she had just hoped to put it off for another few weeks.

Logan flipped back the corner of his comforter and stood up. Prissy took in his bare feet, the dark whorls of hair covering his long legs below athletic shorts, the soft gray t-shirt hanging from his broad shoulders, the disappointment in his blue gaze.

Same old, same old, then.

"Do you need the bathroom first, or can I have it this time?"

It took a moment for his question to penetrate the fog she was in. His tone implied she was a nuisance, in his way though she did her best *not* to be, which made her declare, "I need it."

He shrugged and strolled out to the main room.

Prissy took care of her morning routine on autopilot.

When would the phone call from her parents come? What excuse could she give them? She had planned to find a husband on the show and present the outcome as a love-at-first-sight fairytale. That, they could understand. This, a marriage of convenience to a man who made bears look friendly, they would never accept.

She came out of the bathroom still panicked, fully dressed except for her shoes, which she carried to the main room while he swapped places with her. He had already made a pot of coffee. Maybe caffeine would help settle her nerves?

She was in her chair with a cup in hand and a plate of toast on the table when he emerged wearing a pullover sweater and jeans that flattered his impressive physique.

She shouldn't look. He was a jerk to her most of the time. Handsome is as handsome does, she reminded herself, but it did no good. If Logan Shaw was an ice cream flavor, she'd want to eat the whole quart. He was that delicious looking.

"What are you staring at?"

Huh? She snapped her gaze up to his and felt her face heat. Instead of answering, she stuffed a piece of toast into her mouth.

"I'm heading up to Littleton later. Do you need to go shopping for anything?"

"Mm-hmm," she mumbled around the mouthful of toast.

"I'm going out for a couple of hours. Be ready when I get back."

LOGAN HAD NO REASON to go into the office on the day before Thanksgiving, and nothing needed his attention at the restaurant.

Crazy as it seemed, he left the apartment to get away from his unwanted wife.

He gave one-word answers to her questions. That didn't stop her from asking them.

She put all her toiletries in that basket under the sink, yet her scent permeated the small space and every morning he breathed her in.

Each time he opened the refrigerator he was reminded she was there.

At night he stepped over her sleeping bag or around it to get to the bathroom, and though she always woke for a minute or two, she didn't say anything. It didn't matter. He could hear her breathing in his sleep.

The only explanation he could come up with for his own behavior and for letting her get under his skin was that he was dog tired. Once they moved into the house, things would improve. He would give her the bedroom furthest from his and they would have separate bathrooms.

By next week, the house would be in turnkey condition. Just like he had promised Dummer. He forced himself to think of his brother, to remember that he wanted Logan to raise his child, and Cherilyn's parents' unreasonable conditions for him to claim that privilege. He and Cherilyn had spoken on the phone once after the restaurant meeting. She said she knew the child would be better off with him than anyone else and that she would support him if, and when, a showdown between them happened. He thanked her but knew he couldn't rely on her.

She was young. Easily influenced by her parents. In mourning. Dealing with loss and pregnancy hormones at the same time. Dummer had loved her, but they had their ups and downs. They broke up every six months, then got back together again. In Logan's mind, that made her just like the other women in the Shaw brothers' lives. Those who they should most have been able to count on all said one thing while doing another.

That's why he had to keep his walls up with Prissy. She might be ditzy, but she was also tempting. And temporary. He reminded himself that she was a gold-digging college drop-out. It didn't help as much as he hoped.

He would just have to treat her like a roommate. Someone he co-existed with who happened to be an attractive female.

Resolved, he drove back to the apartment.

She was waiting at the bottom of the staircase and opened the truck door as soon as he pulled to a stop. He could say, thanks for not keeping me waiting, or, sorry I was an insensitive jerk—again—this morning, but instead what exploded out of his mouth was, "What the hell are you wearing?"

"You're baaack," she sang in her little girl's voice, probably referring to his manner more than his appearance. Then she hopped in and scooted across the seat, closed the door and reached for her seatbelt. The movement drew his gaze to her legs, encased in ribbed black tights, too much of their length showing between a red plaid skirt and her combat boots.

It shouldn't have been a sexy outfit; it was smoking hot.

"Answer me," he said, forgetting his mental pep talk about co-existing and treating her like any other roommate. "What do you think you're wearing?"

She glanced at the thin black sweater, skirt and tights. "Is this a trick question?"

Logan could feel steam building in his head and knew he was one wrong word away from blowing his top. Taking a deep breath to calm himself, he bit out, "You look like a schoolgirl, for crying out loud. Go put something else on."

Her hands stilled on the seatbelt. Her gaze was steady, her answer succinct. "No."

That was it. The one wrong word.

"I am not taking you out dressed like that." Her scent in the bathroom, the sound of her breathing at night, her presence, were making him crazy. He could only take so much temptation. "Either you put something else on, or you can stay here, but I will not have people thinking I'm a pedophile."

"You know what? You are not the boss of me."

"Now you sound as young as you look."

She let the seatbelt slide back into its anchor. Fisting her hands on the crossbody bag and black hoodie in her lap, she took a deep breath. Her small chest hardly seemed to move, but her sweater lifted an inch above the waistband of that too short, sexy skirt.

"No one would think you're a pedophile, Logan." Her use of his name had him snarling inside. Because she never used it. And because he liked the sound of it on her porn star lips. "You'd have to find me attractive for that, and we both know you can't stand the sight of me."

He could have corrected her. Instead, he repeated, "Put something else on or stay here."

She opened the truck door. Normally she slid out, thanked him for the ride, and shut it behind her. Today, she leaped out but leaned back into the cab and with a smile of pure saccharine, said, "Enjoy your trip," before slamming the door in his face.

He bought her a winter jacket. In Woodsville she hadn't found anything she liked. In West Lebanon she liked the selection but there were none in her size. So, he knew what that size was, and had some idea of her taste, though he chose a mid-thigh quilted parka over the shorter alternative. To cover her up. To keep her warm, he rationalized, adding a puffy pair of gloves and matching hat to his purchases.

He planned to give them to her the next morning, but she left without waking him.

What was *wrong* with him? He didn't like her. He certainly didn't owe her anything. Okay, he did owe her the same respect he would give to a stranger, yet just when he thought she might be less of an airhead than he first suspected, she got that phone call from her sister.

He was so confused he didn't know which end was up and he had only lived with her for two weeks. At this rate, he'd be in therapy by December.

"You don't have to like her to bang her," Chris said over Thanksgiving dinner.

"Language," Lauren reproved, with a glare because Ricky and Matthew were at the table, both old enough to understand what was going on.

"Who says I want to?" And how did the conversation go there? He had simply been explaining where she was today, not that he had or would have invited her to join them.

"I like her," Ricky announced. "She's nice to everyone at work. Not just customers. Darla is mean to her sometimes, because she's jealous, but Prissy smiles and puts up with her crap. Shelly lets other people get away with not doing everything they're supposed to. Prissy makes sure the restaurant is clean and stocked before she leaves. She helps me if I'm the last one there."

"Maybe you misjudged her?" Lauren suggested when the silence lengthened.

Logan could tell them about the phone call from her sister, about her refusal to buy a car, or a coat that wasn't pretty enough, but none of that explained his behavior. What was a delicious meal sat like lead in his stomach.

He would apologize to her; pick her up from work, offer her a plate of food from this Thanksgiving table, promise to take her shopping tomorrow to make up for yesterday, and say he was sorry for what went down between them.

She wasn't at the diner. He arrived a little before three to find the lights already off and no sign of movement from the kitchen, though he went to the back door and peered inside to make sure.

The road into town was empty. He stopped at Campbell's Country Store, in case she was getting something from the deli, but they had closed at noon for the holiday. He ducked inside the covered bridge and found it empty. None of the other shops on the common were open.

By the time he made it to the apartment, he was seriously worried about her safety. So, when he walked in to find her at the kitchen sink, he sagged against the door with relief. She had to have heard the door open, but she didn't turn around. After their stand-off in the truck yesterday, he wasn't surprised. Then he saw what was in her hands.

"Where did those come from?"

When he was really angry, his voice came out low and quiet.

She went still on hearing that tone. She was a lot smarter than she first appeared.

Slowly turning away from the sink, water still running behind her, she finally faced him.

"Answer me."

Holding up the hapless flowers in her hands, she croaked, "They're from a friend."

Logan swore his vision turned red. "A male friend?"

Her head jerked slightly, like she tried to nod but froze mid-motion.

"Answer the question."

"Yes." Her voice was wispy at the best of times; now it was a mere breath of sound. She cleared her throat and tried again with more force. "Yes, a male friend."

Logan tossed the plate in his hand onto the counter beside her. It bounced against the wall, the foil cover coming loose, a pile of turkey and stuffing spewing out over the lip of the plate like vomit.

"Do you remember what you agreed to in the prenup?"

"It's not—"

She didn't finish because he braced his arms on either side of her, leaning in until his mouth was at her ear. He could feel the blossoms in her hands being crushed between their bodies. "No men in your life. Period."

The next day he came home to find every surface in the apartment covered with flowers. They were on the counters, the windowsill by the sink, the back of the toilet, the table by her chair, the corners of the bedroom. If he wanted to know how she felt about his edict, there was his answer.

Refusing to react to the profusion of blossoms stinking up his apartment, or to the challenge in her eyes, he said, "I found a car for you. Be ready to look at it after work tomorrow."

He was still congratulating himself on his non-reaction when she came out of the restaurant the following afternoon. He had even rationalized his behavior.

His mother had sold herself to pay for her addictions. Not on a street corner or using an eight hundred number, but she hopped from bed to bed and house to house, taking advantage of a number of men, dumping him at a young age with his aunt who raised him until she and her husband had their own child, then returning him to his mother until the State of New Hampshire finally intervened. He had no respect for women who traded on their good looks that way. Prissy had done that by entering the reality show.

As his wife, even a mostly secret one at this point, she was a reflection of his character. He wouldn't have her taking up with other men on the side and damaging the reputation he had worked years to build.

That rationalization went up in smoke when she came out of the kitchen. Because instead of making her way to his truck, she walked to the corner of the building and blew a kiss— a freaking kiss!—to a man getting into his car at the edge of the parking lot. Then she sashayed over to his truck and climbed into the passenger side as if nothing had happened.

"Who is he?" Logan growled, unable to contain his anger.

"That's Gil." She smiled and waved at the other vehicle as it left the lot. "My friend."

"Your flower friend?"

She clicked her seat belt in place and turned her full attention to him. "Yes, Logan," she said slowly, as if speaking to a toddler. "He is my friend, and he gave me flowers for Thanksgiving. That doesn't mean I sleep with him. It is possible for a man and woman to be just friends."

Not likely. Not when the woman had silky caramel hair, big brown eyes, and a porn star mouth. Yet if he said something, he'd have to admit she wasn't hard to look at. Or that he cared. He threw the truck into gear and pulled out of the parking lot.

"We're going to Jamie's garage," he said a few minutes later, pleased his voice was back to normal. "He doesn't sell cars, but he has a customer who planned to trade hers in or sell it, so he asked her if we could take a look at it."

"Is it within my budget?"

"She wants twelve grand for it."

"I don't have twelve thousand dollars."

"I know. If it's a good car and you can't get it for less, I'll lend you the extra. You can pay me back when you get your check in six months."

"Six months less two weeks, you mean."

As if he needed a reminder.

In the meantime, he'd just think of her like a roommate and do his best to keep her out of his life as much as possible.

Easier said than done.

Jamie was showing the little station wagon to them when his younger brothers came out of the house across the yard. "Hey, Prissy," Ricky greeted, "this is my brother, Matthew."

"Well, of course he is," she smiled, her wispy little voice disarming and charming as she continued, "and just as handsome as you."

"Jamie's the big brother," Matthew added, as if she was overlooking the most handsome of the three, but his cheeks were pink, his eyes glazing over with puppy love.

Great. Just what Logan needed.

"The car?" he reminded everyone.

Jamie produced the keys and offered them to Prissy. "Do you want to take it down the road and see how it feels?" His garage was at the end of a long dirt road with two other homes on it. "Maybe go to the A-frame and back?"

"Yes, but I need to know if it's comfortable for passengers." She glanced at the boys. "Would you two like to come along with me?"

Logan couldn't object without looking like a jerk, so he remained silent, only thinking of the insurance implications of her driving someone else's car with minors after the taillights disappeared at the end of the driveway. It would have made a good argument.

Beside him, Jamie raised his eyebrows and said, "You need to chill."

Chapter Eight

Prissy bought the car and had it registered and inspected by the end of the next week. That process created something of a dilemma because she needed an address for the paperwork. She also had to decide what name to put it under.

"Twenty-one Dunlap Mountain Road," Logan supplied with obvious reluctance when she asked him about this before going into the town clerk's office. "But use Schermerhorn."

"The clerk issued our marriage license," she reminded him.

"Lots of women keep their maiden name. She'll just think you're independent."

Shrugging, because it would be easier this way than registering the car under one name and changing it later, she did as he suggested.

Back in the truck again, she said, "Your apartment isn't on Dunlap Mountain Road."

"No." He drove out of the municipal parking lot and up toward the town common.

"Are you ever going to show me this house you bought? I thought we were moving in a week ago."

"There was a delay with the flooring. And I've been too busy to give you a tour. I do work for a living, you know."

Prissy took a calming breath when she really wanted to poke him in the side, preferably with something sharp. Instead, she said, "I know you're busy. You're never home. I assume you're working on this place at night?"

"Day and night."

"And are you ever going to tell me what you do for work?" She had suspicions, after Darla and Thalia's conversation at the diner, but she couldn't ask them for details without explaining her interest in him.

Sighing like she was asking a lot, he said, "I'm a partner in the sand and gravel business."

That explained why he walked right in the day of their wedding as if he owned the place. Because he literally did.

"And I'm the managing partner at A Notch Above."

"The restaurant where we filmed scenes for the show?"

He nodded, yielding at the common to another vehicle before turning onto the ring road.

Prissy glanced idly at the covered bridge, Campbell's Country Store, and Kelly's What-Not Shop while absorbing this news. "So, you weren't really working as a security guard?"

"I was."

Okay, she'd have to pull a few teeth to get more out of him. "Explain it to me."

"Explain what?" he asked. She was certain he was being deliberately obtuse, so it surprised her when he continued. "I bought the restaurant last year. The previous owners had a contract with the show's producers, so I honored it because a lot of local businesses were going to benefit from having the cast and crew here this fall."

They passed the North Country Trading Post and the road to the transfer station.

"Our chief of police died unexpectedly just before filming began. The contract called for security during film shoots, so I stepped in because I didn't want the town sued."

"So, you're also a cop?"

He shook his head. "Not anymore. I worked as one for a few years when I was younger."

The side road leading to his apartment flashed by. "Where are we going?"

"To twenty-one Dunlap Road."

She hadn't expected that answer, but at this point she added it to the pile of surprises. He was a business owner. Not just one business, but two and, from what she had seen, both were successful. Who *was* this man? And why did he marry her? She had been so grateful at the time, despite his rude behavior, that she hadn't stopped to ask questions. They both needed money. They both got money out of the deal. It had seemed that simple.

Then they left town and drove up Dunlap Mountain Road and she saw the house for the first time. A gleaming white colonial with towering maple trees at each corner presiding over acres of land with views in every direction. She might have thought they were in the wrong place if not for the granite post at the end of the driveway with the number twenty-one on it.

"You did not need my ten thousand dollars for this," she accused.

"Yes, I did. And it's my ten grand. I'm the one putting up with you for six months."

"Deflection."

"Excuse me?" He had the nerve to sound outraged when she was the one who had that right, because nothing about him was adding up the way it was supposed to.

"You're deflecting. Ten thousand wouldn't be enough for a down payment on a house like this."

"Don't forget I also worked security detail for the show."

"There's still something you're not telling me."

"We're going to a dinner party tomorrow night. Wear something nice, but not too fancy."

"Excuse me?" It was her turn for outrage.

"Be ready at five o'clock. I'll introduce you as my wife, but don't say anything about how we met. And don't even think about wearing that schoolgirl skirt."

She ignored that order. "I thought you didn't want anyone to know about us."

"Yeah, well, things change. One of the witnesses assumed we'd had time to share the news by now. It was an accident. So, the cat is out of the bag, and I have no choice but to bring you with me. Just remember, don't say anything. Smile, and keep your mouth shut."

That did it! "I am not a dog or your slave. If you want my help, then you'd better start treating me like an equal, or I won't go."

"Yes. You will."

"You're forgetting that I don't owe you anything." She had been honest with him, only now realizing she knew next to nothing about the man.

"This isn't a negotiation."

"I'm aware of that. If it was, you'd have some leverage, but you need me for this, not the other way around. So, it looks like I'm the one with all the power this time."

"Should I call your parents and tell them you bribed me to marry you?"

She closed her mouth.

Her stomach knotted with worry, because when her parents phoned after her sister's message, she let their call go to voicemail. Cowardly, she knew, but she had run away to another part of the country, to a television reality show, to avoid telling them the truth and nothing had really changed since then.

By their third call, they threatened to contact the police if she didn't answer, so she called back on a Sunday morning, when they would be in church and their phones on silent mode.

"Hi, Mom and Dad. It's me. Sorry you had to find out this way, but I fell in love and, you know, just got carried away. Like Grammie and

Grampa." She used that comparison because her mother's parents had fallen in love at first sight, so they would have a hard time arguing she couldn't have experienced the same thing. It still didn't explain going on the show in the first place, but she ignored that.

"I'll call you back and fill you in on all the details later." Like the fact that she married the man? Probably not. "Okay, I've gotta go. Love you."

Her phone had been blowing up every day since then. Her little sister texted to say their parents were losing their minds. Her older sister asked where she was, just in case there was an emergency, and someone needed to find her. Prissy shared her location after getting a promise from her sibling that the information would stay between the two of them.

Her parents' calls continued. They were angry, which was understandable, but they were also disappointed, which crushed her and at the same time kept her from calling them back. How could she ever explain that after years of planning, and years of support from them, she simply changed her mind about her future career?

She finally sent a text promising to call this Saturday afternoon.

Instead, Logan told her to be ready for a party by five and, uncertain how high- or low-brow that might be, she asked Gil for advice on what to wear.

If she could share her marital status with the women at work, she'd ask them, but since it was a secret she had no one else to turn to. Logan certainly wouldn't give her his friends' numbers—Ivy or Lauren—and regardless of what he thought, she didn't want to embarrass him.

"Understated, of course," Gil said. "We don't like anything grand in New Hampshire."

Like an apartment filled with flowers? Check.

"And it has to be practical. Women here don't suffer the cold to look good."

So, no high heels. That left her combat boots and slip-on sneakers.

He must have seen the dilemma on her face. "Do you need to go shopping?"

"Are you offering to go with me?"

She really didn't want to give Logan another reason to be angry with her, but he was the one who assumed Gil was a young man on the make, which was his problem, yet he had insisted she dress up, which was hers.

"I'll drive."

She hadn't been to Littleton before. Gil showed her the box and chain stores, the charming shops on Main Street, and his late wife's favorite destinations.

Prissy found an oatmeal sweater dress at a small boutique and a pair of faux leather boots with braid trim at the shoe store, and all for less than two hundred dollars. She'd love to brag about that to Logan, but then she'd have to explain the tortoiseshell ring and earrings that cost almost half as much. It was one thing to dress practically, but she couldn't forfeit all good taste.

She asked Gil to drop her off beneath the streetlight on the corner just in case Logan was home, then breathed a sigh of relief when she saw the yard was empty. That meant she had the bathroom to herself. Not wasting any time in case he should come in before she was done, she pleated three tiny braids at each side of her temples and merged them into one bigger braid at the back of her head. Her makeup was minimal; mascara, a smear of dark shadow in the crease between browbone and eyelids, and a dusting of bronzer on her cheeks. Lip gloss was a must.

The dress looked good, what she could see of it when twisting and turning in the bathroom doorway to see her reflection in the mirror above the sink, but she didn't like the knit belt. Made of the same fabric as the dress, it hung limply from where she knotted it at her waist.

"This will never do," she decided, and raided Logan's closet for a solution. She had almost given up finding anything when she saw the tongue of a leather belt sticking out between two folded pair of pants. It was several inches longer than she needed. No problem. Using the metal prong, she poked a new hole in the leather. The loose end dangled from the buckle, so she secured it with a chunky wooden bracelet. This put the buckle at one hip, the bracelet at the other.

Maybe she'd start a new fashion trend.

Adding the jewelry she had purchased in Littleton, she donned her new parka, tied the hood securely at the neck, and was just picking her gloves up when Logan came home.

"Ready?"

"Yes, sir."

"Don't be a smartmouth."

Since she was only being polite, and it had never occurred to her he might take offense, she stuck her tongue out at him, but he had already turned to open the door, so he missed it.

Or so she thought. "I saw that."

Of course, he did. The man never caught her doing something good.

He also never volunteered information, so when they were halfway to Woodsville and he hadn't said anything else, she broke the silence. "Tell me about this party."

"Nothing to tell. Remember, you're just supposed to look good and keep quiet."

"Arf, arf, master."

His lip curled up with the beginnings of a smile before he seemed to remember who she was and that he didn't like her. Pressing, and knowing she was pressing her luck, she asked, "Are you going to pet me and give me a bone if I perform well?"

That hadn't come out exactly as she planned. He must have interpreted it the way it sounded, though, because he went stiff in the driver's seat, and she could have sworn she heard him gnashing his teeth. Well, good. She might not have meant anything sexual by her remark, but for three weeks she had been living with glimpses of his hard body and it was getting to her. She woke each time he came home and couldn't fall asleep again until he finished in the bathroom and dropped to the mattress. The sound of his breathing was her own personal lullaby.

She also liked his scent. Sometimes she picked his pillow up and held it to her nose, closing her eyes and imagining what it would be like to lie on that mattress with him. She also wondered how she was going to survive six months when she was banned from having other relationships but turned on by the man least interested in having one with her.

Logan cleared his throat. "It's a regional development group. Businesspeople, politicians, movers and shakers. We meet four times a year to plan and coordinate marketing efforts. In the summer we have a golf tournament to raise money for scholarships. In the winter we have this holiday get-together."

"Will your business partners be there?"

He nodded.

"Chris, and Jamie?" She clarified just in case there were any more secrets up his sleeve.

"Ivy, too. She's not a partner, but she's a member of the group."

"And they know about us? Your partners, I mean?"

"They know you bought me as a husband."

He didn't speak again until they were parked on a vast common surrounded by colonial homes with long windows casting yellow rectangles of light on the snow.

"Remember what I said?"

"Yes, master. Look pretty and keep my mouth shut."

He let out an exasperated sigh.

"I'm not an idiot," she grumbled, "I can act when I need to." The doubtful expression on his face looked almost demonic in the blue glow of the dashboard lights. "Did you really think I was attracted to the men on that show?"

LOGAN CONSIDERED HER comment. She went on a few dates and flirted with several of the men, but if he was honest, he never saw any real chemistry between her and the male contestants. Yet on camera it looked real. So, he gave her the benefit of the doubt and said, "Okay. Let's go. Our hosts are Martin Vanderpool and Kathy Schmidt. They're Dartmouth professors, married, he teaches business, she teaches pediatric medicine."

When she made no comment, he asked, "Got it?"

"Yes, master."

"Keep that up and I'll drop you off at the pound."

They crossed the road to a three-story colonial high above the Connecticut River. Single tapered lights glowed in every window. A large evergreen wreath hung above the front door, and tiny white lights framed that rectangle. It was all understated and regal.

Logan pulled the brass knocker twice and stepped back to wait.

He wondered what Prissy was wearing beneath that long black coat and kicked himself for not checking before they left. She was pretty good at getting her own back when it came to their confrontations, so he wouldn't put it past her to pull a retaliatory stunt. Too late to worry about it now. He just hoped she didn't embarrass him.

The door opened. "Logan. Come in, come in," Martin greeted, ushering them into the wide foyer. "And who is this, all bundled up for winter?"

Putting a hand to the small of her back, Logan said, "This is my wife. Priscilla."

They exchanged greetings, then Martin showed them to a small coat closet beneath the staircase. "We're just down the hall on the right. Join us when you're ready."

Logan shed his coat and adjusted the collar of the button-down shirt he wore beneath a thick cabled sweater. He slipped off his duck boots and retied the laces on one of his leather shoes while Prissy hung her coat in the closet.

Half expecting the plaid skirt or something tight and silky, he was pleasantly surprised by her appearance when he rose from tying his shoe.

A buff-colored dress clung to her figure. It was modestly cut, with a high neckline and long sleeves. Her silky blond hair had been braided and pulled back in a simple style. Unlike the heavy makeup she wore on the set during filming, tonight's was light and flattering. Simple gold and tortoiseshell jewelry added a touch of class to the look.

She was still sexy, he accepted now that she could be dressed in sackcloth and get a rise out of him, but not in the same way as when she got into the truck for their aborted shopping trip. Tonight's brown boots and thick leather belt—

"Is that my belt?"

She smiled and winked at him.

Doorbell chimes echoed off the walls around them.

Martin came into the foyer and grinned. "A host's work is never done."

Following his earlier directions, they passed the staircase and entered a formal dining room on their right. Conscious of the role he was playing, Logan placed his hand at Prissy's lower back where his belt was cinched around her small waist. In a low voice close to her ear, he said, "You helped yourself to my closet?"

If she answered, he didn't hear her because Kathy Schmidt saw them and let out a surprised, "Prissy Schermerhorn, what on earth are you doing here in New Hampshire?"

Logan didn't get a chance to ask her about that until they were in the truck on their way back to Ammonoosuc Falls. "You have some explaining to do."

"Why?" She pulled her hood close around her face. He'd noticed that when it was cold, her voice lost power, and he could barely hear her over the sound of the heater slowly warming the truck's interior. "Because I raided your closet? Or because you wrote me off as an airhead and now you've figured out I'm not one?"

He'd known that for a while, but things still weren't adding up. "You went to Tulane." The Ivy school of the South. He thought her sister said something about college during their phone call, but maybe he hadn't heard correctly. "You didn't finish?"

"I graduated with a baccalaureate degree in biology. Summa cum laude."

So, she was book smart. "Then why were you in that reality show? You don't seem desperate for a man."

Those words hung in the air for a prolonged moment. He pictured her tight rear end in soft clingy shorts as she disappeared into the bathroom each morning. He remembered that sliver of soft skin between the hem of her sweater and the top of that sexy plaid skirt. He recalled the moment of silence between them in the truck on the way to tonight's party.

What was she thinking now? Did it have anything to do with petting, or a bone?

"I told you, I need the money," she finally replied, her voice having gained some volume.

"Are you pregnant?"

"No." A definitive answer.

"A gambler?"

"No again." This time she sounded amused.

"Are you going to tell me why you need thousands of dollars, then?"

"No. That's my business."

"I don't want any surprises."

"Well, bully for you. If you can have your secrets, I get to keep mine."

Chapter Nine

Hers were waiting to be exposed when they returned to his apartment.

"What have you done?" Logan demanded.

"Me?" she cried, as surprised as he was to see the state police cruiser parked at the bottom of the staircase with its blue lights flashing. "I haven't done—

Her defense stopped mid-sentence when a couple she recognized stepped out from behind the police vehicle.

"Something you want to tell me?" Logan bit out.

No. She really didn't want to. Half tempted to ask him if they could turn around and drive off, go anywhere else, she swallowed the lump of dread clogging her throat and whispered, "Those are my parents."

Logan turned off the ignition and killed the headlights. When he didn't open his door to get out, she met the challenge in his hard blue gaze. "Time to grow up and face consequences."

Prissy's stomach dropped. She hadn't expected any support from him but left to her own devices she would have run away. Since that's what got her into this mess in the first place, she took a deep breath, unbuckled her seat belt and opened the door.

"That's her," her mother said to the police officer standing beside the patrol car. "That's our daughter."

The three of them approached, looking Prissy over for what she suspected were any signs of harm, or mental illness.

"Priscilla Schermerhorn?"

The policeman didn't need to use that stern voice. He was a threat simply by being armed and uniformed, but her parents were the bigger danger.

"That's me," she squeaked, vaguely aware of Logan exiting the truck.

"Your parents have been worried about you, young lady."

For a brief, hysterical moment she contemplated saying, *That would explain why they're fifteen hundred miles from home.* Instead, she bit her lip to keep the words inside and nodded.

"They thought you were at school in Austin, Texas. Can you explain how you came to be here in Ammonoosuc Falls? And why you haven't been answering your phone?"

She nodded again, then realizing he waited for a verbal reply, said, "Yes, sir." He and her parents eyed her expectantly. "I came here to participate in a television show."

"That doesn't explain anything," her father groused.

The officer's suspicious gaze landed on Logan, now standing a couple of feet away. Prissy dared a glance in his direction. His stance was casual, his expression neutral, his eyes furious. At her? Or at the police officer?

"And are you here of your own accord?" that officer asked.

Swallowing fear, shame, and an unreasonable feeling of abandonment, she said, "I am."

"You weren't coerced?" Doubt laced his tone. "You aren't in danger?"

"No, sir."

"Please get into the cruiser."

"No." Prissy stumbled backwards, away from him.

"I only need to ask you a few questions. Alone." His gaze fixed on Logan. "To ascertain that you are here of your own free will."

Now she was exasperated. "I'm of age, sir, and I haven't committed any crime." She glanced over her shoulder at Logan. "And, as far as I know, neither has anyone else here."

The officer looked to her parents, his eyebrows raised in question. "I can leave you to sort this out—" he tilted his head toward Logan —"or stay if you want me to."

"Thank you, officer." Her father shook the man's hand. "We'll take it from here."

"I'll be off, then." He touched his fingers to the brim of his hat as a goodbye to her mother, got into his cruiser, and drove away.

They listened as the hum of the patrol car's engine grew smaller and smaller until it was swallowed up by the night and stillness descended on their little tableaux. The lack of sound weighed as heavily on Prissy as the dry winter air, seizing her lungs and robbing her of voice. She shivered despite the warmth of her new coat.

For the first time, she noticed the gold sedan with Massachusetts plates parked on the other side of the yard. Her parents must have rented it from whatever airport they flew into. She studied the car as if by doing so she would find answers, guidance, or escape.

Logan finally broke the awkward silence. "Maybe we should get out of the cold?"

Latching onto that suggestion, she said, "Yes, please."

Her parents followed her up the stairs, Logan behind them. It wasn't until they were inside that she remembered how pathetic the apartment looked, an almost empty main room with nothing to soften the stark interior but the last remaining vase of week-old flowers.

Prissy came to a stop in the middle of that barren space. Her parents stood a few feet away, together, united while Logan leaned against the door. Despite his presence, she had no illusions of a partnership between them. She was on her own.

Her mother threw out the opening salvo. "Explain yourself, Priscilla."

Falling back on good manners, she said, "Maybe we should take off our coats? You can sit—

Her suggestion died out because there were only two chairs in the apartment.

"This is not a social call, Priscilla Daphne Nicole." Her mother cast a quick glance at Logan. "I can see how you might have got carried away—a backhanded compliment about his looks—but now it's time to face reality." She tugged at the wrists of her gloves as if putting them on. "Go and get your things. Your father and I will wait for you in the car."

"No."

Prissy and her parents turned as one when Logan spoke. She wasn't sure which of them was more surprised. While her parents gaped at him, he said, "You asked her for an explanation. The least you can do is listen to it."

Her father's cheeks went ruddy. He was a successful businessman and a born and bred southerner, unused to younger people talking back to him, or to his wife. "Now you listen here, boy. You may think your opinion matters, but this is a family affair, between us and our daughter."

"He's my husband."

Her father's head jerked like she'd slapped him. Her mother gasped and covered her mouth with a dainty gloved hand.

Logan seemed almost as surprised by the announcement as her parents, but he merely folded his arms over his chest and waited.

Her mother recovered first. "Prissy, how *could* you?" Disappointment evident in her tone.

"The hell you say," her father objected. He looked around the apartment, his expression clearly doubting there was anything of value for her to collect, yet he said, "Priscilla, pack your things. We'll sort this mess out when we get home." To Logan, he added, "You'll be hearing from our attorney."

"No, sir."

Her father's complexion went from ruddy to fire engine red. Prissy felt the color drain from her own face. She had never been disrespectful to her parents in her life.

Again, her mother was the first to recover. "Don't talk back to your father."

Prissy flinched, then trembled, but she stood her ground. "I'm a grown woman, Mama."

"Who obviously isn't thinking clearly."

"One whose judgment can't be trusted." Her father waved a hand at their surroundings, as if the apartment was all the proof he needed.

"Mama, Daddy, this is Logan Shaw." Time to show she hadn't completely forgotten her manners. "Logan, these are my parents, John Michael and Augusta Schermerhorn."

"I refuse to accept that."

"If this is a joke, it's in very poor taste."

Prissy continued despite their outrage. "I think we should sit down and talk, but not here and now. If you want, we can meet tomorrow and have an adult conversation." She stressed the word adult.

It went over her parents' heads. They demanded, then argued, and finally resorted to soft persuasion with a lot of honeys thrown in, but she held firm. Even if she wanted to jump into that gold car and go home where it was warm, and colorful, and safe, nothing about her financial situation had changed. Lying to them about her relationship with Logan was better than telling them the truth.

"Please. I promise I'll explain everything, but it's late, and you must be tired from your trip," she said. "Mama always says things look better in the morning, right?"

"How could they look any worse?" her father glared at Logan.

"Daddy, please don't insult my husband."

"Don't call him that."

Her mother tried a softer approach. "I'm sure this can all be corrected, right, honey?"

"Tomorrow, Mama." Which wasn't an answer but seemed to pacify her for now.

Eventually Prissy saw them out with an agreement to meet at the diner the next day. She listened at the door while their footsteps receded down the stairs and car doors opened and closed, then she turned off the outside light and slumped against the wooden panel.

She couldn't face Logan. While he hadn't offered much support tonight, he also hadn't corrected her parents when they assumed he took advantage of and somehow coerced her into marriage. He could have defended himself and told them about the marriage bribe. He could still use it against her now. Instead, he hung up his coat and asked, "Do you want to use the bathroom first?"

Such a normal question. Like they hadn't just spent half an hour listening to her parents impugn his honor and question her sanity.

She jumped at the chance to escape.

THE PRISSY WHO EMERGED twenty minutes later looked nothing like the confident woman Logan had picked up earlier that evening. Gone was the makeup, the braids, the oatmeal dress that flattered her trim figure. She wore an oversized, long-sleeved polo shirt buttoned up at the neck, a miniscule pair of shorts, bare feet with pink polished toes, and an air of defeat that made her look young and small. Avoiding his gaze, she rolled out her sleeping bag and waved to the bathroom. "It's all yours."

The light was off when he came out. Like every other night, he walked past where she lay and dropped onto his mattress, plumping the pillows and pulling the comforter up to his waist, then listened for her breathing.

A hitch of sound. Silence. Another hitch. When he realized she was crying, something inside his chest turned over.

This woman-child had never backed down from anything and certainly never accepted defeat. Determination might as well have been another middle name to her. First she showed up at his apartment with her crazy proposition, then returned the next morning to pitch her idea again with revised terms. She got a job the day they were married. She held her own against him when it came to spending money, and bringing home flowers, and keeping secrets.

At the diner she charmed the working class. In Woodsville she conversed with ease among business owners and academic elites. Plaid skirt and black tights notwithstanding, she was polite, polished, demure, and entertaining. Listening to her cry, now, made him uncomfortable.

He hadn't wanted a wife. He certainly didn't have room for one in this apartment, but he didn't hate sparring with her as much as he once had. Even a week ago her crying wouldn't have bothered him. Tonight, it did.

"Prissy?"

"Hmm?" Her voice was a muffled thread of sound.

"Come here."

"What?"

"I said, come here."

Her sleeping bag rustled. Her bare feet pattered across the wood floor and her dark silhouette came to a stop beside his mattress.

She sniffled.

Flipping back the corner of the comforter, he reached for her hand.

She tried to avoid his touch. While her resistance was commendable, he overcame it with one firm tug, and she fell to her knees beside him. He eased her down onto a pillow and pulled the comforter up over the two of them.

Though she lay stiffly at his side, he felt her body quiver with tears.

"You did a good job tonight," he said. "Everyone liked you."

A sniffle of sound escaped, but she relaxed slightly.

"You looked nice, too."

She rolled toward him.

"I liked the dress, even if you did wreck my belt to wear it."

A soft exhale of breath fell against his arm.

"I don't know where you got it, but it was pretty."

She tensed slightly before whispering, "Gil took me shopping for it."

Logan pushed her face into the notch between his neck and shoulder. "Shut up and go to sleep."

Despite that order and her best makeup efforts, she left the apartment the next morning with red-rimmed and crusted eyes. He had already been awake for hours, listening to her soft breathing and wondering how he got himself into this mess.

Unable to sleep even after she left for work, he spent a few hours at the new house accomplishing nothing before finally giving up and driving to the Chiswick Diner.

Her parents were already there. By the looks of their table, they had been for a while even though the agreed upon meeting time was almost an hour away.

Logan slid onto an empty counter stool.

"Coffee?"

He hadn't heard her come up behind him. He turned the mug over on the placemat in front of him and nodded, observing, "They're early."

"That's my dad's signature move."

He raised his eyebrows in question, and she grimaced. "He thinks it gives him the upper hand. That means I'm an adversary, and he's not here for a conversation."

"I can take it from here, Prissy," the dark-haired waitress interjected, sliding behind the counter and coming to stand in front of him. She offered him a menu and a dazzling smile. If she leaned in any closer, her big breasts would sweep the countertop. "Just let me know when you're ready to order."

"Thank you.

"I think I'm going to throw up in my mouth," Prissy mumbled while walking away.

Logan grinned. The woman certainly didn't pull any punches.

His humor didn't last long. The other waitresses, Darla and Thalia according to their nametags, were obviously fighting. They exchanged glares and barbs every time they came within a few feet of one another. One swiped ketchup from another one's table, one emptied the coffeepot and didn't start a new pot brewing, tables went uncleared, and a rack of clean glasses sat waiting to be unloaded on a tray beside the kitchen door.

While they scored points off each other, Prissy ran the length of the dining room, took and delivered orders, refilled condiment jars and coffee cups, and smiled at everyone despite her obvious fatigue.

He had a better understanding of Ricky's Thanksgiving Day comment now. When his nephew came out of the kitchen to fill a glass with soda from the fountain, Logan called him over. "Where's the boss today?"

"She sprained her wrist." Correctly interpreting Logan's glare, he said, "It's not always this bad." He took a drink of the clear bubbly liquid from his frosted glass and added, "I'll help her clean up if she needs it."

"You're a good man, Ricky."

The crowd began to thin out after that. Prissy cleared and wiped down tables, put the clean glasses away, and served a big slab of mincemeat pie and coffee to a latecomer. When he and Logan were the only diners left besides her parents, they motioned for Prissy to join them.

Her shoulders sagged and she slid onto the banquet seat beside her father. Logan threw a few bills down on the counter for his coffee and got to his feet.

It was hard to say which of them was more surprised when he took a seat next to her mother and across from Prissy, but he couldn't let her do this alone.

Darla almost chased after him only to stop short on seeing who was at the table. A comical mix of expressions crossed her face, confusion, irritation, then anger. She was smart enough to connect dots and had probably already gone from Logan giving Prissy a ride home that day to him sitting down at the booth with her as if he belonged there.

"Do you folks want your check?" she snapped.

"Just leave it on the table." Prissy's father said without glancing her way. He leveled a look at Logan which plainly said he wasn't welcome at their table.

Logan ignored him, caught Prissy's eye, and gave her a subtle nod.

She took a deep breath and sat up taller in her seat. "I know you have a lot of questions—

"Damn right we do."

—and I'll answer them but let me explain first."

She stopped and wiped her palms against the bib of her apron. "I signed up for the reality show on a lark. You know, if finding love at first sight was good enough for Grammie and Grampa, I figured it could work for me." Her voice lost volume and she clenched her fists on the tabletop. Logan reached across that surface and covered them with his hand.

Her startled brown gaze met his. He squeezed her hands. Relaxing slightly, she continued with her story. "Anyway, that's how we met. Logan was helping the town out, working security for some of the scenes, and he was just so *nice*," she laughed, and he marveled at her acting ability because he had never been nice to her, "and the rest is history."

"But what about your future?" her mother asked, seeming to soften just a little. "What about medical school?"

"I don't want to be a doctor." She was shaking like a leaf, and her voice quavered, but she didn't apologize or back down. Logan had to respect that.

Her father didn't see it the same way. "You're giving up on your dreams?" he exclaimed. "After all those years of hard work? You just met this man."

"It's not that, Daddy. I knew at the end of the first year that medicine wasn't for me."

"But your grades?" Her mother seemed baffled. "You were doing so well."

"To make you happy. I wanted you to be proud of me."

Her father's face fell. "Why didn't you say something? We could have talked this out."

Logan had his doubts about that, but he remained silent. He also withdrew his hand from her fists because she seemed to have this under control now.

They stopped talking when Darla dropped off the bill. Prissy's father handed her fifty dollars and waved her off. Her mother waited until the waitress was out of earshot before leaning across the table to say, "Dropping out of medical school is one thing. Marrying a stranger fifteen hundred miles away is something else entirely." She glanced uneasily at Logan before adding, "He doesn't even have furniture in that apartment. How do you expect to live?"

"And this," her father swept his arm out to indicate the almost empty restaurant, "is not the kind of job we want for you."

Darla was back with their receipt and change. Prissy's father missed the daggers she shot on hearing his opinion of her occupation.

"Thank you," her mother said, as if to make up for that, "the food was excellent."

"Well?"

Prissy's cheeks were pink. Logan didn't know if that was from her father's brusque manner, him putting down her job, or Darla witnessing the confrontation. He had no doubt the other waitress was now standing inside the kitchen trying to listen in on their conversation.

"Logan has businesses," Prissy defended, "and there isn't any furniture because he's moving into his new house this week."

"*He* is?" "*His* house?"

"We are," she corrected, "and it's beautiful. I could show it to you?"

"No."

All three of them turned at Logan's declaration.

"You don't have to prove yourself worthy of their approval," he said to Prissy, keeping his eyes on her parents. "If they're worried about your safety, or comfort, that's one thing, but you're obviously safe and healthy. You don't need to impress them for their sake."

Both parents reared back in their seats. Logan wasn't sure what was coming next. Anger? An explosion? Accusations?

Her mother teared up. "Honey, is that what you think?" She covered her mouth with one perfectly manicured hand as if holding back a sob and her brown eyes filled with tears. "Prissy, we love you just for you."

"Thank you, Mama."

Her father narrowed his eyes and stared at Logan for several long seconds. Both a challenge and an inspection, before moving his gaze to Prissy. Whatever he saw there made him relax back against the banquet seating. "Your mother is right," he conceded, "you know we love you more than rainbows."

That must have been a special saying between them, because Prissy's brown eyes now glistened to match her mother's. "Thank you, Daddy. I promise I know what I'm doing."

Both parents smiled, and he wondered what it was like to have people care this much and worry so much they hopped on a plane and came to the rescue.

A shadow fell across their table.

As one, they looked up to see a tall, gaunt man whose smile of greeting revealed a spiderweb of wrinkles across his gray-tinged complexion. "You must be Prissy's parents." He extended his hand to her father, who shook it.

Prissy rose, and he didn't have to wonder long at the mischievous gleam in her brown eyes. "Mom, Dad, Logan, this is my friend Gil Peringer. He owns the local funeral home."

Chapter Ten

"Think you're pretty funny, don't you?" Logan asked when she arrived at the apartment after him.

"About what?"

"As if you don't know. Letting me think Gil was some random guy flirting with you."

She took her time hanging her coat on a peg. When she glanced his way, her eyes sparkled. "Well, he *does* like to flirt."

That surprised a chuckle out of him. "I think my little wife might enjoy it, too."

"I'm not going to apologize," she said in a prim voice. "You're the one who jumped to conclusions."

"Guilty."

"I'm sorry, I must not have heard you correctly."

"Don't be a smartmouth or I'll take it back."

This time she laughed, and he realized he'd never seen her this relaxed before. It seemed like the right opportunity to ask the question that had been eating at him. "Prissy, why did you ask me to marry you?"

She was quiet for some time. Not normal, the woman really was a yapper, which told him how important this decision had been for her. "I have huge student loans from medical school. Since I'm not going to be a doctor, I'll never have the big income to pay them off. To be honest, a lot of doctors don't, either, but I couldn't see any way to have a life of my own with them."

That surprised him because it showed she had given the problem a lot of thought and come to a rational decision, even if her solution was irrational. "You could file for bankruptcy and start again."

"Student loans are exempt from bankruptcy."

He hadn't known that. He had earned his degree on nights and weekends while working full-time and paying for the tuition himself.

"The reality show seemed like my best chance."

"Hmm." He considered her situation, and her solution, for a minute. "But I could have been a psycho. I might have strangled you in your sleep."

She chuckled. "You mean you haven't thought about it?"

"Touché."

She went to the refrigerator and took out a quart of orange juice, poured herself a glass and held the carton up in question.

"No, thanks."

She returned the container and leaned against the counter with glass in hand.

"Is the money going to be enough?" he asked. "For you to start a life, I mean?"

"It would have been, but..."

"But now you have to share it with me."

She took a sip of juice before saying, "It gets me a lot closer than I was. Now I'll have the equivalent of an expensive car payment instead of a small mortgage."

A twinge of guilt nagged at him, but he refused to let it grow. She was the one who offered him this deal, and he was putting up with her for six months, even if that was no longer the burden it had once been.

"Logan?"

"Hmm?"

"Are you going to tell me why you accepted my marriage proposal?" When he didn't answer immediately, she pressed. "You didn't need my money—" she held her free hand up to forestall him correcting her—"I know, it's *your* money."

He rolled his shoulders and questioned the wisdom of sharing his situation with her. On the one hand, she might talk to customers at the diner, and he didn't need everyone north of Franconia Notch knowing his business; on the other, she would find out what was going on in about eight weeks, anyway, and he would need her support.

"I had a little brother," he explained. "Dummer. He would have turned eighteen the day we got married, and he was going to come and live with me."

"Was?"

"He died that week."

"Is that why you were drinking the night I showed up?"

He nodded. "His funeral was that morning."

"I'm so sorry."

He didn't respond. Lots of people were sorry, but it didn't bring his brother back.

"So, what does that have to do with the money?"

Taking a risk, knowing this might cost him, he said, "His girlfriend is pregnant."

Prissy's lips formed a perfect O of surprise.

"She didn't tell Dummer when she first found out, because he was sick. We thought it was just epilepsy at first. She planned to tell him later."

"What was it?"

"Gioblastoma."

"So, there was no later."

"No." Logan swallowed the hard lump in his throat, but his voice was still hoarse when he continued. "She's just a kid, not ready to be a mother. She told Dummer before he died, and he wanted me to raise the baby, but her parents want her to put it up for adoption."

Prissy's mouth tightened and her normally soft eyes blazed with heat. "Show me to them."

"What?"

"I mean it. It will be my pleasure to unload a can of whoop-ass on these people."

Logan laughed out loud. He could get used to this, talking with her like they were partners instead of combatants. "That won't be necessary. Ivy got a court order preventing them from putting the baby up for adoption. When the baby is born in two months, I'll be bringing him, or her, home with me. But just in case they challenge me for custody, I figured it was better to be a married man."

"Hmm." Finishing her drink, she placed the empty glass in the sink. "Logan?"

The hesitation in her voice made him wary. "Yes?"

"Do you have other family?"

"No."

She gave him a soft smile and said, "You do now."

He appreciated the comment almost as much as her non-reaction to his situation. If people weren't condemning him for being abandoned, they gushed with sympathy, both serving to remind him he was alone, yet Prissy seemed to take it in her stride.

"What now?"

"Now I've got to take a shower. I told my parents I'd meet them at their bed and breakfast and spend some time with them. It's in Lincoln. How do I get there?"

Logan provided directions while privately wondering if she'd be back tonight. Would they pressure her into returning with them to Florida? That's what a lot of parents would do in this situation, yet when he got home from work her caramel streaked mane spilled out over the top of the sleeping bag. She hadn't run off.

Standing over her, he listened for a moment to the reassuring sound of her breathing.

She was awake when he came out of the bathroom.

"Hey," he greeted.

"Hi." She rubbed her eyes, squinting against the bathroom light, and he reached back in and flipped it off.

"Everything go alright?" "How was work?"

"You go first," she said when they both paused.

"Quiet," he answered. "Things slow down a little bit between now and Christmas."

"Is that why there was no food in the apartment when I first moved in? Because you eat there?"

Logan crossed the room and settled onto his mattress. "That, and the move."

"Good. I'd hate to think you live on beer alone."

Grinning, he punched the pillows behind his head and pulled the comforter to his waist. "How did things go with your parents? I see they decided against kidnapping you."

"Yesss," a prolonged hiss of sound.

"Yes, what? I think I hear a but in there."

"But they'll be back."

"Oh?" A moment ago, he had been relaxed. Now he tensed and waited for her explanation.

"They're flying home tomorrow, but they're coming back for Christmas, and they expect to stay at the house. Dad's words."

"I have a room," Logan sighed. So much for an uncomplicated relationship. Now he had in-laws and, though they turned out to be caring parents, he wasn't eager to spend more time with them. Keeping up a charade for an hour or two was one thing, pretending to be a happily married couple for an extended period of time would be a challenge.

"My sisters, too."

"Come again?"

She flopped down on her sleeping bag. "Mama said it might be nice, having a white Christmas, and if I was determined to stay here, and since there was no wedding or reception, we could all celebrate the holiday together."

"Hell."

"Hmm."

Logan punched his pillows again, taking his frustration out on them because they were available. "How many sisters?"

"Two. One older, one younger."

"And what are their names?"

"Lulu and Muffy."

Logan scoffed at the ridiculous monikers. "Your parents should have raised poodles."

Prissy giggled, finally bringing a smile to his face when she said, "Arf, arf, master."

THEIR ACCORD LASTED less than forty-eight hours.

"I think we should have a housewarming party." They were at his house, had been unpacking boxes all afternoon, and this was their first break, her first chance to pitch the idea.

Logan took a long pull from a bottle of water and wiped his mouth with the back of his hand. "No."

His automatic refusal neither surprised nor deterred her.

"We should," she insisted. "I can't keep lying to people at work about the two of us, and it's better if we announce it than let them discover it out on their own."

"Have you forgotten what you agreed to?" he snapped, his loud voice bouncing off the walls of the upstairs room where they worked.

His anger didn't bother her. Since his kindness Saturday night and Sunday, he had been putting distance between them. She recognized it as a self-defense mechanism and didn't take it personally. He didn't want to like her.

Understanding that, she kept her tone reasonable. "No, I haven't forgotten. But when you showed up at the diner, and sat down with me and my parents, tongues started to wag."

"And what did you do to stop them?"

"What should I have done?" She put down her empty water bottle and dug into a cardboard box for the next wrapped household item. "I can't just say, stop speculating. Darla thinks you're the hottest thing since the Chinese invented fireworks." She pulled the packing paper back to reveal a picture of the covered bridge on the common. "Did you really expect her to accept me saying, 'He just needed a place to sit,' when the whole restaurant was empty?"

"Fine." Logan flattened the cardboard box he had just emptied with a little more force than necessary. "We can't keep it a secret from everyone. That doesn't mean we're going to have a party and pretend to be a happy couple."

"Yes, we are." Prissy put down the picture frame in her hand and advanced on him, though she stopped a few feet short, not quite brave enough to get close when he was like this. "Just listen to me for a minute."

"No."

She ignored his reply and the tension in his shoulders. "Your business partners and Ivy know about us. The town clerk knows about us. The bank manager, the people in your business group, my parents, all know we're married and the people at the diner have guessed there is something going on."

"Let them guess. They don't need to know."

"You can't keep this a secret."

"Yes, I can."

Prissy wanted to shake the man. "Think about what you're saying. We can't show my parents around without people guessing. And if you act like I'm a dirty secret, people will wonder why. What's wrong with her? Why did he marry her? Is she pregnant? You need to pre-empt those kinds of questions."

Logan scowled and pulled another box out of the corner, slicing the top open with a box cutter. He turned the cardboard flaps back and pulled out a handful of shredded newspaper. "What makes you an expert on what I need?"

"I'm not stupid." She ignored his raised eyebrows and stepped closer. "You worry about what people think."

"Some people."

"The people in this town. You want their respect."

"They do respect me."

"I agree." She had heard his name often enough at the diner, and everyone had good things to say about him. "But you don't want anything to happen to your reputation, and a hole in the wall wedding that you refuse to acknowledge won't do it any good. And your child? You don't want your niece or nephew growing up hearing gossip about their father's secret wife."

"You'll be gone before they're old enough to hear anything."

That hurt more than she wanted to admit. Ignoring the pain, she said, "Yes, after we divorce. Divorce is acceptable. People don't talk about that the way they do a secret marriage."

"No. No party. End of discussion."

"She's right."

They both turned on hearing Ivy speak from the top of the staircase. Their argument must have become heated, because neither of them had noticed the front door opening, her crossing the foyer, or climbing the stairs.

"Come again?" Logan asked his friend and attorney.

"I said, she's right. It's time to bring this out into the open."

Logan raked his fingers through his hair. He looked like a man under siege, which she supposed he was at the moment.

"Let her organize the party for you. Shut people up before they start speculating."

"I can just tell people we're married without making a big deal about it."

"That won't be enough for Cherilyn's family."

Those words dropped into the atmosphere like a giant boulder. Prissy had never heard the other woman's name, but she knew without a doubt that Ivy was referring to the parents of Dummer's girlfriend.

"Throw a party. Prove yours isn't a marriage of convenience."

Logan glared at both Ivy and Prissy. "There's nothing convenient about it."

"Pizza's here!" Matthew shouted from the bottom of the stairs.

"And so is Ivy." Chris looked up at the three of them standing in the hall above the foyer. "Jamie and Ricky just pulled in behind us. We figured it was time to eat."

Ivy started down the stairs, leaving Logan and Prissy to follow. On the top step he took her elbow and hissed, "This conversation is over."

Prissy had learned a thing or two about her husband. He took offense to most of what she said or did, but he usually relented or came around or at least came to terms with it later. She also knew he wouldn't let her go without an answer, so she winked and said, "We'll see."

LOGAN SHOULD HAVE KNOWN that wouldn't be the end of it. He reached the formal dining room to find everyone seated on cardboard boxes, passing around pizza and drinks, discussing his housewarming party. Prissy didn't even have to contribute to the conversation. Ivy had taken the lead, and when Lauren dropped in with Emmy, the whole thing mushroomed beyond his control.

"I can help you with the invitations," Lauren volunteered, patting her very round belly. "I should have some free time soon."

"I wouldn't want to put you out," Prissy objected. "You'll be busy."

Lauren waved her argument away. "Not too busy to make a list for you."

"And, of course, A Notch Above can cater the event. Right, Logan?"

He barely managed a halfhearted grunt in response to Ivy's question before they were rattling on with plans, managing his life for him. A life that seemed to be spinning out of control, first with a wife, then in-laws, and now a housewarming party with half the town on the guest list. By the time they finished eating, he was resigned to hosting the event.

"It will be fine," Ivy assured him while collecting empty cups.

"It will be fun," Lauren added, rising to her feet but only halfway. "Jamie!" She gasped, clutching the mantel behind her.

Jamie dropped the pizza boxes in his hand and rushed to her side. Ivy discarded the cups and hurried to get Lauren's coat. Ricky pulled Emmy out of the way as Chris made a beeline for the front door, saying, "I'll pull the car around."

Jamie accepted the coat from Ivy and helped Lauren into it. "Are you okay?"

His friend's wife didn't scare easily. Proven when she smiled bravely and said, "Hope the roads are clear between here and the hospital. This is going to be a fast one."

She wasn't kidding. Three hours later Logan's phone buzzed, and Jamie's number lit up the screen. He rolled off his mattress and went into the living room to take the call. Despite his irritation with her earlier in the evening, Prissy had worked her buns off at the house, unpacking, putting things away, and cleaning where they dirtied what had already been cleaned by the professional crew he hired. She would have to be up at five and he didn't want to wake her.

"Tell me the good news," he said to his friend.

"A boy. Healthy, seven pounds four ounces. Strawberry blond hair just like Emmy when she was born."

"Is Lauren okay?"

"She's a champ. Sleeping now, though."

"I'll bet."

"Wanna know his name?"

"Sure." For some reason, they had been secretive about their choice this time.

"Christopher Logan Campbell."

Logan didn't know what to say. The three of them had been through a lot together, had stood up for one another on multiple occasions, but this was unexpected.

"You know this means you're a godfather, right?"

Jamie's question released the emotion clogging Logan's throat. "I'm in," he said.

"Have a good night, brother."

"Same."

Logan stared at the phone until the screen went dark.

As a child he had been shuttled from house to house, with and without his mother, looking for guidance from the variety of men she slept with but finding no permanent home. If it hadn't been for Chris and Jamie, he didn't know how he would have survived without turning into an unredeemable juvenile delinquent. They stepped in when Cora died. They stepped up. Their friendship kept him sane, and grounded, and helped him become the man he was today.

"Everything okay?"

The wisp of sound came from the bedroom doorway. He couldn't see Prissy, but he imagined her standing in her oversized shirt and tiny, short shorts.

"Everything's good," he said. "Lauren had a baby boy. Christopher Logan."

"Nice name."

"Hmm." He palmed the phone and moved toward the bedroom. She pattered across the floor to the other side of the room where her sleeping bag lay. When they were both settled in for the night, he asked, "When is your next day off?"

"Friday."

"We'll go shopping then."

"Okaaay," she said in a wary voice. "Is there a dress code for this trip?"

Logan smiled in spite of himself. "No plaid skirts."

"And are we looking for anything in particular?"

Conceding she had a point earlier was easier to do in the dark. "We'll need furniture in the guest rooms since your family is coming to visit. And maybe a few other pieces if we're going to have a housewarming party."

THE TRIP WAS A MARATHON event. For one thing, they couldn't find everything in one store, so they had to shop at multiple outlets. For another, they argued over almost every piece.

He made the mistake of telling her he didn't have unlimited funds, which she took to mean he didn't want to pay full price for anything.

"That's outrageous," she told an Ossipee saleswoman after being quoted the price for a dining room set. "For that much money, it should have gold trim and red velvet seats."

"I like it," Logan said. The set had simple lines and good craftsmanship.

Prissy rolled her eyes at the saleswoman. "Men. I swear they don't know how to spell the word budget." Winking at him, she said, "That's B-U-D-G-E-T, in case you're wondering."

He was so taken aback by her talking to him that way, and in front of a stranger, that by the time he came up with a reply she had accomplished her goal.

"You said you are first-time homebuyers?" the saleslady asked, and at Prissy's nod, "I think we have a special discount program for people like you."

In West Lebanon she charmed a blushing young salesman until he agreed to sell three mattresses for the price of two and throw in a body pillow as a thank you for their business.

She haggled at length with the furniture store owner in Hanover, finally getting the delivery charge for their new beds cut in half since, in her words, he only had to go up the river to Ammonoosuc Falls.

"Remind me never to negotiate with you," Logan said when they left St. Johnsbury with mirrors, vases, and other large decorative items for pennies on the dollar.

"You already have," she reminded him, scowling at the memory, "and you made out pretty well on that deal."

"I did?"

"Fifty percent is a lot more than my first offer."

"Yes, but look what I have to live with," he mock sighed.

She stuck her tongue out at him.

He grinned and turned on the radio.

"This is more like it," she said when they arrived at the salvage store in Lisbon.

Logan looked through the windows at a crowded collection of discarded items from other people's homes. "You have a problem with new furniture?"

"No, but it can't all be new."

He disagreed. As a child, he lived with hand-me-down clothing and used toys. As an adult, he preferred things others hadn't already touched, and he never went into stores like this if he could help it. "Remember, we're just looking for a print for the foyer bathroom."

"Uh-huh." She unsnapped her seat belt and slid out of the passenger side.

"Prissy," he warned, getting out and coming around the hood to join her, "You said you wanted a Johnson's Baby Powder or Ivory Soap ad to frame."

"Don't worry."

The wink should have warned him. Half an hour later she stood in front of a grandfather clock with an ivory face and giant gold pendulum. The thing was taller than he was.

"It's a statement piece," she argued when he asked why she wanted it.

"And what, exactly, is the statement?"

"That your home has permanence."

"You don't think the age of the house already says that?"

"No. Just imagine this clock, between the closet and the staircase. People will see it when they enter the foyer. Imagine hearing the chimes upstairs every hour, on the hour."

"I'd rather be sleeping when I'm upstairs, not have this thing going off."

"Don't be a grump."

"Excuse me?"

A customer passed behind them and she paused until the man was out of earshot before continuing. "Logan, you have a beautiful house. I want to showcase that beauty for you. Why are you arguing about this?"

He was dog tired, that's why. He'd been moving furniture all week from where it was stored at the sand and gravel building, working nights at the restaurant, and today they stomped all over two New Hampshire counties and half of eastern Vermont. Instead of saying any of that, he simply gave in. "Get the damn thing."

Her smile full of victory, she grabbed the information tag from the clock and marched up the aisle toward the counter. Halfway there she stopped with a gasp.

Logan teetered on the balls of his feet behind her, arms pinwheeling until he could regain his balance and avoid crashing into her. "What *now*?"

"You've got to get this."

Looking over her shoulder, he saw the wicker bassinette she pointed to.

"What for?"

Giving him a look that clearly said, duh, she nonetheless explained, "For the baby."

"Chris?"

"Not Jamie and Lauren's baby." Lowering her voice to a whisper, she said, "Yours."

Chapter Eleven

Gil came in early the next day and stayed late. He ordered chocolate cream pie with his coffee, but asked Prissy to deliver it when she would have a few minutes to sit and visit.

"So, this Logan?" he asked when she slid into the booth across from him.

Cheeks hot, she admitted, "He's my husband."

"You didn't stay for the scenery, then? Or, maybe for a different type of scenery?"

If she were any more embarrassed, she'd burst into flame.

"You love him."

Prissy opened her mouth to object, then closed it. Denying Gil's statement would lead to more questions, and although she considered him a friend, she owed her loyalty to Logan.

"You don't have to answer, I can see it on your face."

He cut another bite of pie off with his fork and said, "I've got flowers in the car for you."

"Oh, good. We just moved into the, I mean, *our* new house, and I'm decorating."

"Saying it takes some getting used to?"

"It does."

"Do you like decorating?"

Did she like it. No. "I love it! I have so many ideas," and although she and Logan disagreed about some of them, he was letting her have pretty much free reign even though it was his house and she'd be gone by summer. Swallowing the pang that came with that thought, she said, "Any recommendations for where I might get a sewing machine and some fabric?"

His rheumy blue eyes lit up at her question. "I have a room full of sewing supplies."

"You do?"

He nodded. "My wife was a 4-H sewing instructor. We couldn't have kids, but she taught other people's children how to sew. She judged the Fashion Revue and everything."

"She sounds amazing."

"She was. She would have liked you, too, and she would be glad to see her equipment in good hands. Do you have time today to come by and look at it?"

Grinning, she said, "Just as soon as my last customer leaves."

Half an hour later she signed out and followed Gil to his funeral home on Route 302. The yellow stone building had stained glass windows, a white columned portico entrance on one side and a larger matching one on the other side for hearses. Gil pulled into the parking lot at the back of the building, below a similarly colored home on a slight knoll above them.

"You live here?" she asked when they were both out of their vehicles.

He nodded, leading the way up a wide set of steps to the house. "Born here, too."

The interior of his home was almost entirely visible from the front entrance, a large main room holding the kitchen, dining and living areas, and two open doors on one side revealing a bedroom and what was obviously the sewing room.

It was a treasure trove. By the time she left, her car was bursting with a sewing machine, needles, a wall rack of fifty thread spools, scissors and other tools, but the best part was a trunk full of fabrics.

Until her parents came to visit, she was sleeping in a small anteroom at the end of the hall. It was square, and light, with one long window facing the back lawn and a view of the Ammonoosuc River. On the opposite wall a long rod gave evidence to this being a dressing room at some point. A door on one side opened out into the hall, on the other a pocket door gave access to the master bath.

Prissy set the side table Logan had bought her for the apartment beneath the window and set her new machine up on top of it, then went to work.

She spent every afternoon sewing. By the end of the week her fingers were bruised, and her shoulders hurt from bending over the machine, but there were new placemats in the dining room and matching drapes at the windows.

Their furniture arrived a few days later. Logan put the beds together, a queen in his room and a double bed in each of the guest rooms, and Prissy went back to sewing.

She ordered supplies and materials online. Within days the bedrooms and living room had window treatments. She made throw cushions for the sofa, her favorite piece of furniture after living in the apartment without one.

Next, she tackled the anteroom. Its size and location made it perfect for use as a nursery, so she started by painting the clothes rod white. From that, she draped white fabric decorated with adorable woodland animals in muted grays and greens. She pinned the drapes to the sides of the opening and put the bassinette between them. A cozy little alcove for Logan's baby.

She was full of ideas for the rest of the room, but those would have to wait until she made the rest of the house presentable.

LOGAN NOTICED THE EVIDENCE of her labors all around him. The farmhouse table and benches in the kitchen had been stripped of gaudy yellow paint, sanded and scoured to reveal the wood grain beneath. A speckled blue and white tin bowl in the center of the table held fresh apples and oranges.

Floral placemats in the adjoining dining room picked up the same blue color, and though they were a different print from the curtains, the mismatch worked.

The main rooms were homey and welcoming. Fresh and dried flowers were artfully arranged throughout the house, guest soaps and pretty towels in the downstairs bath beneath a Norman Rockwell print of kids bathing a dog in a round metal tub.

A giant wreath adorned the front door. Evergreens with red bows lined the fireplace mantel and wrapped around the stair railing, making the red berries pop in the wooden bowl on a table next to the grandfather clock.

She was right about that purchase. He loved seeing it on entering the foyer, and he didn't hate the sound of the chimes. For the first time in his life, his home brought comfort.

He wanted his child to experience that same sense of security. As soon as Christmas and the housewarming party were over, he'd have to think about getting one of the bedrooms ready for the baby. Through texts with Cherilyn, he knew that everything was right on schedule. The baby was big, but neither she nor Dummer had been little, so the doctor wasn't concerned.

His one worry stemmed from her parents. They had gone from encouraging her to give this child up, hiding its very existence from him, to suddenly wanting a role in its life. Cherilyn thought they wanted to make up for their mistakes in raising and spoiling she and her brother.

Logan didn't want them anywhere near his child, but if push came to shove, he'd let them be part of its life because every child deserved to have grandparents.

"Something on your mind?" Prissy asked, stopping halfway down the staircase when she saw him standing in the middle of the foyer.

"No." He shook his head to clear it. "You said your sisters are coming in tomorrow?"

"Yes. I'll have to pick them up at the airport."

She bit her lip and her brow wrinkled.

"If you're worried about the drive, I can go with you."

"Really? That would be wonderful!"

She slept all the way to Manchester. He didn't rouse her until they arrived at the mall. "What are we doing here?"

"We need rings. Your parents didn't say anything, but I saw them looking at our fingers."

She nodded but didn't speak. A sure sign of fatigue that might otherwise worry him. He hoped it meant she'd be too tired to argue with him in the jewelry store.

No chance of that. This ring was too big, this one was too expensive, this one was the wrong cut. He finally pulled her away from the counter and hissed, "What, exactly, would make you happy?"

"Logan, those rings could pay for a quarter of my car! And it's ridiculous to spend that much on something that's temporary."

"Your family doesn't know that."

"Well, I'm not spending that much, and we'll never get it back when we sell them later."

"Who said you're paying for them?"

"We split everything, fifty-fifty, remember?"

Logan ran a hand through his hair, frustrated yet not surprised that this was turning into a fiasco. A glance at his watch showed they had little time to finish up here and meet her sisters' incoming flight. "Hold on. Let me talk to the salesperson and see if we can make a deal."

"I'm better at negotiating than you are."

"Prissy...." He almost growled the warning.

"Okay, okay." She held her hands up in surrender. "Let's see what you've got."

She complained all the way to the airport. "That was not fair. You shouldn't have bought them without me, and I didn't agree to even half that price."

"I paid for them."

"No way. You'll have to add it to my tab." She groaned miserably. "I already owe you for the car."

Logan's short fuse was long gone, but he didn't say anything else until they were parked inside the airport garage. Then he turned and took her by the shoulders, saying, "The rings are a gift. You can sell them for whatever you want later, but for now, just shut up."

"Shut up!" she sputtered. "Did you just tell me to shut up?"

He almost laughed at her indignation. "Your sisters' plane arrived two minutes ago."

She yelped. Then he did laugh when she scrambled out of the car and ran across the short-term parking lot, forcing him to jog after her. She only slowed down at the main entrance to the airport because the door was one of those circular things that forced her to wait her turn.

"Do you know where you're going?" he asked when she bypassed the screen inside that showed flight departures and arrivals. "Or what you're looking for?"

"You can't miss them." She bounced on the balls of her feet, craning her neck to see around the crowd, in direct contradiction to her statement. "They're almost as tall as you."

"What do they look like?" He could see over most of the people in the airport terminal. If he didn't help her look for them, she might break her neck trying.

"Tall. They got Dad's height and Mom's blond hair. Her beauty, too."

That comment surprised him. Prissy was an attractive woman, with her caramel streaked hair, elfin face, and tempting lips. Even Chris acknowledged she was easy on the eyes. He wondered what she saw when she looked in the mirror.

"They're here!" One second, she stood beside him, the next she squealed and rushed toward the escalator, waving frantically to a pair of women descending from the upper level.

Wow. Despite her description, Logan almost did a double take along with every other man in the vicinity. Far from the poodles their names suggested, these women were supermodel sleek, blond, and towering over almost everyone around them.

"Prissy!"

The few people who hadn't been following their progress turned at the happy shriek.

"I'm so glad you're here." "I can't believe you did this!" "Is it always this cold?"

They all talked at once, laughing, hugging, and moving in his direction. When they stopped in front of him, arms linked at the elbows, Prissy beamed, "Logan, these are my sisters."

"I'd never know."

She wrinkled her nose at his dry comment, and he half expected her to stick her tongue out at him, but instead she continued with the introductions. "This is my big sister, Ada Luella Louise Schermerhorn."

The woman on Prissy's left gave him a cool smile, her gaze narrowed suspiciously. "So, you're the guy who convinced my little sister to give up on all she ever dreamed of."

"Lulu!" Prissy gasped.

Logan stiffened, ready to defend himself but not getting a chance before the other sister dropped Prissy's elbow and stepped forward to wrap him in a surprisingly strong hug. "Hello, big brother." She kissed his cheek and stepped back to look him over, blue eyes dancing with mischief. "Welcome to the family."

Prissy sighed. "This is my baby sister, Mary Margaret Dawn Schermerhorn."

"Muffy for short," her sister added. "And aren't you something." Leaning down, she whispered in Prissy's ear, sotto voice so he could hear every word, "Are there any more like him? I want one."

"Do stop it," Prissy scolded, slapping her sister lightly on the arm. "Logan will think the two of you don't have any manners."

"Well, we can't have Logan thinking poorly of us, can we?" Lulu interjected, neither a question nor a compliment in her tone.

"Don't be mean to my husband." Prissy dropped her sister's arm and reached out to take his. He tried not to show his surprise, because Lulu was watching him intently and she didn't need another reason to dislike him.

"Do you have luggage to collect?"

Muffy laughed. "Is the Pope Catholic?"

"Let's go and get it, then. The longer we spend in here, the colder the car will get and the two of you aren't used to this weather."

The ride back to Ammonoosuc Falls was long and noisy. Prissy spent most of it turned sideways in the passenger seat so she could see her sisters behind her, the three of them chatting almost non-stop. He learned that Lulu worked in marketing for a luxury hotel chain in Miami and Muffy was on her third college major, one semester away from a degree in liberal arts. He hadn't known anyone granted general degrees these days.

"Do you think you'll ever pick something?" Prissy teased.

"I don't know." There was no apology in her tone.

"You could always run away and join a reality tv show," Lulu suggested.

Ouch. Was she always nasty, he wondered, or just overprotective of her little sister?

He didn't have long to wonder.

Lulu was waiting for him in the kitchen when he came downstairs the next morning. She wore dark lounge pants, a faded Miami Dolphins t-shirt, and flip-flop sandals. Her hair was thrown into a messy bun, her face was clear of makeup, and she was just as gorgeous as she had been the night before.

He didn't mistake her appearance for casual, though, any more than he believed she just happened to be up at this hour after traveling the previous day. She had been lying in wait for him.

"Would you like some coffee?" he felt compelled to ask, crossing the room to the pot Prissy made each morning before leaving for work.

"I've already had some."

Okaaay. He poured a cup for himself, added sweet cream from the refrigerator, and leaned back against the counter. He could start this conversation or wait for her to make the first move. He waited.

Several long seconds passed.

Logan drank from his mug and checked the weather forecast on his phone.

"What is the deal between you and my sister?"

He didn't look up. "We're married."

"You might feed the parents a love at first sight fairytale, but I'm not buying it."

He didn't bother to deny or confirm the story.

"Prissy doesn't do anything spontaneous."

That got his attention. "Come again?" Most of the decisions she made were straight from the heart with little rational thought to them.

"Everything Prissy does is for someone else."

Logan took another drink of coffee.

"Why did you marry her?"

"Why do most people get married?" he countered.

"Don't try your lines on me. I'm no fool."

She might be beautiful, and her soft drawl might give an impression of warmth, but this woman had none of her sister's sweetness. He almost had the urge to check his back and see if there were claws there that needed retracting.

"My sister had her whole life planned by the time she was seven. Then, after the cancer, she replanned it. Every. Last. Detail."

Logan was too stunned by this news to respond. Prissy had cancer?

"When she left in August to go back to medical school, you were not in the picture, now suddenly she's married to you?"

"Except she didn't leave for medical school," he pointed out, still processing the news about Prissy's childhood illness.

"No. Instead she pretended to be there, then joined that reality show. The one where couples get a hundred grand if they stay together for six months."

Logan raised his eyebrows. "You've done your homework."

"Of course I have." She narrowed her gaze, "I'm a smart woman, and Prissy is my little sister. She has spent her whole life trying to make up for being sick."

"Say what?" He couldn't have heard her correctly.

"For getting cancer. Our parents sold off two of their businesses to pay her medical bills, and they still ended up filing for bankruptcy. She thinks she owes them for that."

"She thinks Muffy and I were cheated out of attention, because she needed so much from everyone. She's always trying to fade into the background, to give us center stage, if you know what I mean."

"She wasn't hiding on that reality show."

"Exactly. So I know my sister, and I know she had a reason for doing what she did. I'm just trying to figure out what it was, and how you fit into the picture."

"There you are!" Muffy bounced into the room, at least as much as a woman just shy of six feet tall can, walking right up to Logan and embracing him in a tight hug. Completely unselfconscious despite being dressed in a skimpy pink lace bralette and matching short shorts. She glanced between him and Lulu, put her hands on her hips and said, "You haven't been interrogating him, have you?"

"Of course I have."

Muffy rolled her blue eyes and just for a moment she reminded him of Prissy. "Well, cut it out. We've got a brother at last, and I don't want you ruining our first Christmas with him. Besides, you need to get dressed so we can go to the diner."

"Me?" Lulu's voice was filled with exasperation. "You're the one half naked!"

"I can change that."

Before Logan could guess her intent, Muffy grabbed the hem of her bralette and yanked it over her head.

He averted his eyes to avoid catching a glimpse of something he shouldn't see.

"There," she challenged, "Now I'm almost completely naked. Is that better?"

Logan dumped his coffee out in the sink and headed for the door. "I think I'll leave now."

"Relax. She's wearing sticky buns."

He didn't turn around.

Chapter Twelve

Prissy was nervous. Excited. Terrified. All those things, when she arrived at A Notch Above. Logan had asked her to join him at the restaurant by seven. Okay, to say he asked was a stretch, he more or less ordered her to be there if she was, 'determined to tell everyone about them,' and those *were* his exact words. So, she put on her oatmeal sweater dress, borrowed his belt again, and presented herself with her sisters at exactly seven o'clock for her debut appearance as his wife.

"Do you have a reservation?" the hostess asked politely.

"She doesn't need one." Logan came out from behind the rock maple bar adjacent to the lobby and slid an arm around Prissy's waist. "Cara, meet my wife, Priscilla, and her sisters Ada and Mary."

"Your *wife*?" the woman's jaw dropped, though she recovered quickly. "I didn't even know you got married!"

"We were waiting until her family knew before telling the rest of the world," he explained, lightly tucking Prissy's arm against his side, looking for all the world like a happy newlywed when he gazed into her eyes. "It wasn't easy, though. As you can see, I hit the jackpot with this one."

Cara extended her hand. "It's nice to meet you, Priscilla."

Stumbling internally, she accepted the woman's handshake. "You, too, but please, call me Prissy."

Logan waved a hand to indicate the dining room on their right. "I've got a table for you." Guiding her to a table in the corner by the fireplace, he held out a chair for her and she slid onto the smooth wooden surface, surprised to find her legs were shaking. Here was the charming man with good manners, the one she witnessed while filming the show, the one she rarely saw when they were alone together.

She was afraid of this one. She could easily fall for him when he was like this, and in just under five months he'd be filing for divorce. She needed to keep her eyes on the prize, which was the fifty thousand dollars, so she could start a life of her own without impossible financial obligations. The last thing she needed was a broken heart.

"I'll be joining you, but until then you can expect all the staff to stop by for an introduction. Do you think you can handle it?"

She nodded, too ruffled to speak.

Lulu took the chair opposite from her, while Muffy waited for Logan to pull one out for her. When he obliged, she gave him a peck on the cheek, and he gifted her with a smile so dazzling it made Prissy's head swim.

"I've got a couple of things to do in the kitchen, but Jessie will be by to take your order." He squeezed Prissy's shoulder in what looked like an affectionate gesture. "Are your parents driving here in their rental car?"

"No." Her voice came out as a nervous croak, so she cleared her throat and tried again. "They were tired after flying into Manchester, then driving all the way up here. They're going to stay home tonight."

"That's a shame." He managed to look disappointed by their absence. She hadn't known he had this much acting talent. "I hope they got settled in okay?"

"Are you kidding? They *love* the place!" Muffy said. "Mama said the bath was heavenly, and Daddy was having a beer in front of your wide screen tv when we left."

"I'm glad," Logan smiled.

Determined to protect herself from this charming man, Prissy accepted a menu from him and buried her nose in it. "Don't let us keep you from whatever you need to do in the kitchen."

Her sisters couldn't see his smirk when he swooped in and gave her a kiss as if he found her hard to resist. "I won't be long."

"Take your time," she said a little too quickly, "We'll be fine."

Except she wasn't.

He had driven the three of them to Littleton for Christmas shopping that afternoon, holding her hand throughout the excursion as if he couldn't bear to let her go. At home he touched her shoulder, ran his hand down the length of her hair, kissed her goodbye when he left for work. When he joined them at the table, his hard, warm body was so close it sent tingles down her spine.

Prissy didn't know how much more of this she could take, and her family visit had barely begun.

"What was that?" Lulu asked.

"Huh?"

"Logan asked how you like your salad, and you muttered something."

"I did?" She looked blankly at her sister, then at Muffy and Logan who were both giving her quizzical looks. "Sorry, it's nothing."

"That's okay." Logan patted her knee beneath the table. "Are you enjoying the salad?"

"It's fine." He raised his eyebrows in question, and she added, "It's delicious, thank you."

It could be cardboard for all she knew. The rest of the meal was the same. Beautifully presented, and probably cooked to perfection, yet she didn't taste a single bite.

By the time the meal ended she was almost jumping out of her skin every time Logan touched her, and he touched her a lot. "Don't you think you're overdoing this a little?" she hissed when he helped her on with her jacket.

"Now, darling, what kind of newlywed would I be if I didn't see to your comfort?"

The twinkle in his eyes said he was enjoying this. Well, two could play at that game. Stretching up on her tiptoes, she clasped his cheeks between her mittened hands and kissed him. The first kiss she had initiated, and she didn't let go when he started to pull away. Instead, she wrapped her arms around his neck and pressed against him.

"Maybe you two should get a room?"

Lulu's dry comment reminded her they were in a public place with an audience.

Logan stiffened. Prissy blinked and dropped her arms. His heated gaze met hers, and she couldn't tell if he was angry or as lost as she was, because something had changed with that kiss.

"Ready to go now?"

"Sorry about that," she murmured to her sister, still tasting him on her lips, still unable to look away from him. She was in real trouble.

"That's okay." Muffy came to her rescue. "If I had someone like Logan, I'd have a hard time controlling myself, too. Are you sure you don't have a brother, or something?"

Logan stiffened, but only Prissy noticed before he exhaled and glanced at her sister. "No brothers," he shrugged apologetically, and at Muffy's pout, added, "But you'll be meeting one of my single friends at tomorrow night's tree lighting."

"What's his name?"

"Santa Claus."

Muffy laughed, but his comment gave Prissy an idea. "Let's go home and watch a Christmas movie. Lulu, you get to pick."

Her older sister had a fondness for British holiday films, and since they were at least a half hour longer than their American counterparts, it should still be running when Logan got home. Prissy could use it as an excuse to avoid going upstairs with him right away.

They were sharing a bedroom while her family visited. Not like at the apartment, where she slept on the floor across the room in her sleeping bag, but tonight and for the next several nights they'd be sleeping in the same bed. She didn't know if she could survive full body contact with him without losing her mind.

"Sounds like the husband's home," Lulu announced halfway through the movie and way too soon for Prissy's nerves. She had been worrying so much over their sleeping arrangements, she hadn't heard the kitchen door open.

Then he was there in the living room archway, shoulder propped against the frame, arms crossed over his chest. Such strong arms. Such a nice chest.

Prissy forced herself to look away.

"Don't you two look cozy." He stepped forward and grabbed a handful of popcorn from the bowl between her and Lulu. Muffy had bailed on them a while ago. "Good movie?"

"One of my favorites, but I think I'll head on up." Lulu removed the fleece throw blanket from her lap and got to her feet. "If I don't, my little sister will take the whole bed. And when I say the whole thing, I mean spread eagle from one corner to the other."

"She is a bed hog," Prissy conceded, while wishing her sister would stay.

"Logan, why don't you take my place?"

So much for avoiding time alone with him. Prissy had no choice but to pat the cushion next to her and smile as if she couldn't wait to cuddle up next to him.

The moment Lulu was out of earshot, she dropped the act.

"Relax." He scooped another handful of popcorn from the bowl. "You're as jumpy as a cat. Keep it up and she'll know something's wrong."

Prissy slumped against the sofa. Maybe she had been imagining his reaction to that kiss at the restaurant. Maybe she was overthinking everything so much she felt sexual tension where there was none?

"The tree looks good." He waved at the evergreen in the corner, which Chris had delivered that morning. She and her sisters decorated it after Logan left for work, so this was his first time seeing it.

"Thank you. I got most of the ornaments at Kelly's What-Not Shop."

"The stars and snowflakes, too?"

"No, I made those."

"That explains why I heard a sewing machine down the hall." He looked around the room. "And these curtains? You made those, too?"

"Yes." Unable to help herself, she asked, "Do you like them?"

He nodded. "But the stockings might be overdoing it."

She had made six felt stockings, three green and three red, each embroidered with someone's name on the white top and further personalized with little adornments. "You don't think stockings are part of Christmas?"

"They are, but the dog theme?" He waved to his stocking, which had little puppies dangling from the white cuff. "What's with that?"

"You bark," she explained.

"Come again?"

"When you're annoyed with me, you bark."

His grin wasn't fabricated, and there was no audience to see it, which made it more powerful and dangerous than any he'd given her today, especially when he said, "And when you're irritated with me, little wife, you say, 'Arf, Arf.' I guess there's a canine theme to our relationship after all."

"You may have a point."

"Come on." Logan stood and, using the remote control, turned off the television. "It's time for bed." She started to object, but he forestalled her by saying, "You were up before the sun, and tomorrow's a big day. You've got to be tired." When she still hesitated, he leaned down until his nose touched hers. "And I may bark, but I promise not to bite."

THE MARRIAGE BRIBE

SHE DRAGGED HERSELF upstairs like a person marching to the gallows. Logan wasn't surprised when she bypassed the bed and hurried into the bathroom. Left to her own devices, she'd probably sleep in the tub instead of joining him in his room.

If she expected to pull off this charade for her family, she was going to have to work harder on her acting skills.

Even his hand at her waist made her tense so much he was amazed no one had called them out on their fake relationship. He didn't know why Lulu hadn't said anything yet, but he was sure she had noticed the tension between them.

For his part, what began as a ruse for her parents' benefit had turned into a game until that kiss at the restaurant. He knew it was retaliation on her part for his overt attention, but the effect that kiss had on him was as real as it gets. He had almost gone up in flames.

He used the bathroom at the end of the hall, between the room her sisters were sharing and the one her parents were in, yet he was still in bed before Prissy finished.

Tonight, she wore full length pajama pants and a fleece turtleneck. The top was evergreen, the white bottoms decorated with Christmas wreaths.

"Someone's feeling festive," he said, hoping she would relax at his teasing.

Instead, she climbed stiffly into bed and pulled the covers up almost to her chin.

Logan turned off the bedside lamp but even in the dark he could feel her lying beside him as stiff as a corpse. He rolled onto his side and faced her. The glow of the alarm clock on the nightstand behind her silhouetted her form and reflected off her open eyes.

"You'll have to do better than this, Prissy."

"What do you mean?"

Her voice was a squeak of sound.

"I mean, you can't act like I'm radioactive and expect your family to believe we're happily married. Which is it going to be?"

"You know which one."

Her reply was mumbled. If possible, her body went even more rigid beside him.

"Then you'll have to act the part." Not giving her a warning, he reached over and clasped her shoulder, pulling her across the space between them. "You've slept with me once before. Did I molest you?"

"No." A tight whisper of sound.

"Did I hog the bed?"

"No." A little louder this time.

"Did I snore like a longshoreman?"

A giggle.

"Then stop thinking so hard and maybe we can both get some sleep. Tomorrow's going to be a big day and I need my beauty rest."

She giggled again, relaxing at last.

As soon as the sun rose the following day, he made a run to the store for doughnuts. Anything to get away from her soft, warm body curled up on the mattress beside him.

His talk last night had been well-intentioned, but he hadn't counted on waking up with her sprawled half across his chest, and although he hadn't changed his mind about the length or nature of their marriage, he was only human. Best to leave before she saw his body's reaction.

Her parents were seated at the table enjoying a cup of coffee when he returned. He joined them with a cup of his own and put the bag of doughnuts on the surface between them.

"Help yourself. They're homemade, delicious, and guaranteed not to clog your arteries."

"Is that the advertising campaign?" her father asked, taking a sugared round and a paper napkin before passing the bag to his wife.

They both murmured their appreciation with the first bite.

"Nothing like them," Logan said. "If you don't get to the store early, they sell out, especially on a day like this when everyone's too busy for cooking breakfast."

He took one for himself and they ate in silence. Morning sun sparkled on the snowbanks beyond the windows and filled the room with light. Crystallized frost on the corners of the glass panes attested to the wall thermometer correctly reading the outside temperature of twenty-five degrees Fahrenheit. He wondered if Muffy managed to sleep through the night without complaining about it.

"Everyone still in bed?" he asked.

"Lulu's in the shower."

Something told him that particular Schermerhorn was probably allergic to sleeping in.

"Tell me about my wife," he said, because that seemed like something a new husband should ask, and they couldn't sit here eating doughnuts in silence all morning.

His father in-law wiped his mouth with a napkin. "What do you want to know?"

"Anything. Everything. Tell me something about her childhood. I'll bet she was a terror."

"No, she was a sweet little girl. And her singing voice! She had the voice of an angel."

Logan supposed any parent would think that of their child but kept his opinion to himself. He couldn't imagine listening to her wispy little voice trying to carry a tune.

"She had so much talent." Her father blinked, moisture gathering in his hazel eyes. "Then she got laryngitis, and the doctors found the tumor in her throat. They said she'd probably lose her voice after the surgery, and we were so scared."

"Not because her singing days were over," he was quick to add, "but because we could have lost her, and even if she made it through, her life would change forever." He swallowed and swiped a hand across his eyes. "A few weeks after the surgery she was able to whisper talk, and I swear I never heard a sweeter sound."

The subject of their conversation came into the room and slid onto a chair between her parents. She had obviously overheard at least some of what they said, because she reached for her father's hand and gave it an affectionate squeeze. "I love you more than rainbows, Daddy."

Logan swallowed the sudden lump in his throat. This is what family was supposed to be. This is what he wanted to give Dummer. They were supposed to have spent this Christmas together, and though Prissy and her family wouldn't have been in his life if things had worked out differently, he could just imagine his brother at the table, scarfing down doughnuts and enjoying their company.

"You were such a fierce little thing," Prissy's mother chuckled, and Logan shook away his heartache to return to the present.

"Remember? You said if Juliette Low could start the Girl Scouts without hearing, you could manage your life without singing." She swung her gaze to Logan and explained, "Prissy was a Brownie at the time. Low was a Georgia girl, like me."

"A Brownie?" Logan asked, all innocence. "They wear the plaid skirts, right?"

Prissy kicked him under the table. He grinned and listened while her mother described the uniform in detail, from the vest to the pleated scooter.

"A lot of the girls wore the white jerseys by then, but Prissy always had a button-down shirt. That way she could hide most of her surgical scars."

Glancing at his wife, he noted the turtleneck top she had on. He remembered the high neck dress on the set of the show, the rolled scarves she wore to work, the sweater dress she bought for the business dinner and wore again last night. Even her hoodies were zipped all the way up and sometimes tied at the top. He wondered now why he had never noticed, while pretending for her parents that he knew all about this part of her life.

"I need to do some last-minute Christmas shopping for Prissy," he suddenly decided. "Will you all be okay if I leave you for a few hours?"

"Of course," her parents said in unison, and he didn't miss the relief that flickered across Prissy's face until he came around the table and gave her a kiss goodbye.

She grabbed him as soon as he returned. Literally, she took his elbow and pulled him into the downstairs bath where she locked the door and turned on the fan.

"What's going on?"

"I don't want anyone to hear us," she hissed.

"And you think *this* is a good place to talk?"

"It was the best I could do. We've got a problem."

"Oh?"

"My parents are asking questions about you. About your family, and who is coming to Christmas tomorrow, and why I don't work at your restaurant as a waitress instead of the diner."

He ran a hand through his hair. They should have anticipated this. "What did you tell them?"

"I said I didn't work at A Notch Above because if I lived and worked with you, I'd lose my independence."

"And they bought that?"

"Yes, because they know I like to do things for myself."

"What else?"

"I told them you didn't have a traditional family, but it was your story to tell. Which made Lulu suspicious, and my big sister is relentless when she thinks I'm hiding something."

He already knew that much about her.

"What are we going to do? Even if they respect your right to privacy, which would be weird since you're part of our family now, they will expect me to know *something*."

She was right. As much as he wanted to keep the past right where it belonged, dead and buried, he hadn't prepared her for familial interrogations.

"Okay. Let me put these away," he lifted the bags in his hand, "then I'll meet you at the truck. If anyone asks, say we're going to pick up some apple pies for tomorrow's dinner."

"Mama has been baking all morning."

"She made pies?"

Prissy nodded.

"Then tell them whatever you want, just meet me outside in five minutes."

Chapter Thirteen

Prissy had seen the many moods of Logan Shaw. Grumpy. That was a given. Charming. Usually with other people. Nervous. Just the one time when they ran into Jamie at the town clerk's office. So when they parked beneath snow-laden tamaracks on a logging road far from the house, it surprised her that he seemed hesitant to speak. His leg bounced against the steering wheel. His eyes darted all around. Minutes stretched into a long period of silence.

"Just tell me what I need to know," she finally said.

He drummed his fingers on the steering wheel. A sheen of perspiration dotted his forehead. This was much more than nervous.

"It doesn't have to be everything," she encouraged, feeling her way because she didn't know what minefield she was dealing with, only that this was new territory for them both. Logan didn't want to let her into his life. He worked hard at keeping her out. Maybe that had more to do with his past than she had suspected.

"Just give me enough to field questions from my sister if she starts prying."

That made him smile. "As if that will stop her."

"You've already got her number."

His smile fell and he ran a hand down his face with a heavy sigh. "I have no father."

"He passed away?"

"I have no idea if he's dead or alive."

She absorbed that but made no comment.

"My mother slept around a lot. I don't know who my father is, not his name, or anything about him."

"She raised you on her own?"

"Ha!"

Prissy recoiled at the venom in his voice.

"Sorry." He fiddled with the heater controls, then dropped his hand to his thigh. "She left me with her sister when I was almost three years old. My aunt Lydia. She kept me until she and her husband had their first child, then she tried to give me back."

"How old were you?"

"Six. I couldn't remember living anywhere else. I thought they were my family."

"You didn't know about your mother?"

"I saw her once in a while, and I knew she was my mother, at least that she held the title, but I was still a kid."

"You didn't understand."

"No. Why did I have to leave for a baby to move in? I said I'd help if they let me stay."

Prissy's heart was breaking, but she didn't think he'd appreciate her sympathy. "So, what happened? One day you lived with them, the next day you didn't?"

"Something like that. After that, I lived everywhere and nowhere. The first time I came to Ammonoosuc Falls was when my mother was sleeping with Jamie's father. We stayed almost a year. Then I was gone for a year, came back for six months, was gone again for a year.

My great grandmother finally took me in, even though she was too old for a kid. Cora Dunlap. She died when I was almost eleven."

"And your little brother?"

"He was a baby, ten years younger than me. My mother said she couldn't handle two kids at once, which was a joke, since she couldn't even handle one kid at a time." His lips twisted and he shook his head, getting himself under control. "She farmed me out to anyone that would let me sleep on their couch. Every few days she'd collect me and dump me somewhere else.

By the time I was fifteen, I was a hellion."

She smiled, but he shook his head at her.

"No, really. I stole stuff. I cut school. I picked fights. A real hellion."

"A scared kid," she whispered, throat swollen with unshed tears. "What changed?"

"The State took me away because my mother wasn't making sure I went to school. They planned on sending me to some people down near Concord, but Jamie's father said I could live with them."

"And that was a good house at last?"

"Yes and no." He shrugged. "His father is a serious alcoholic, but he made sure we had what we needed and got to school every day. And Chris's mother was living with him then, so the three of us were together."

"So, they really are like brothers to you."

"Not *like*. They're the only ones I've ever had."

"Dummer?" Prissy ventured, wondering how all these pieces fit together.

"Jamie's father took me to see him a couple of times a month. As soon as I got my license, I'd go on my own."

"And the house?"

"It was Cora's house. The happiest times in my life were when I lived there."

"Anything else I should know?"

"Ivy's her granddaughter. Cora raised her, so we lived together for a little while."

That explained why the lawyer was willing to write that prenup and perform their unorthodox marriage ceremony without asking too many questions.

By comparison, Prissy had a million questions for him, and she took advantage of this time alone with him to get some answers.

Businesses? They started Jamie's first, then once that got off the ground, the sand and gravel business. "Chris runs the day-to-day operations there, but I'm still the sales contact, since he's not very good with people."

"You're kidding!" she mocked.

"Do you want to know this stuff, or not?"

Birthday? October 17. Age? Twenty-nine.

"Wow, so old," she teased.

Favorite season? Summer. Favorite movie? He didn't have one. Favorite music? Country and rap, both for their story telling. Favorite food? Shrimp.

"Eww! Really?"

"What's wrong with shrimp?"

"It smells."

"Not when it's properly stored and cooked."

"Agree to disagree."

They arrived at the house then, and she had time for one last question. "Favorite color?"

He turned off the engine and glanced in her direction. His answer was so long in coming, she was on the verge of telling him to forget it when he finally said, "Brown."

"What? No one's favorite color is brown."

He shrugged, said, "I like what I like," and got out of the truck.

Snow began falling early that afternoon. They wrapped gifts at the kitchen table with her family while Christmas carols played from a speaker and gingerbread cookies baked in the oven.

"It's like being inside a snow globe," Muffy marveled.

"Wait until you see the common tonight," Logan said.

Prissy had heard about the town celebration from people at the diner, but she was still unprepared for the transformation.

Tiny white lights swept from the peak of the covered bridge out to the lampposts circling the oval. A Bavarian playhouse in front of the store served hot chocolate and gingerbread cookies. At the What-Not Shop, a group of people wearing blue and silver wool capes sang Christmas carols while others toasted marshmallows over a bonfire near the Trading Post. Elves flitted through the crowd passing out candy canes and spreading holiday cheer.

Draft horses pulled a sleigh around the common, the jingle bells on their harnesses adding to the festive atmosphere.

Ammonoosuc Falls was a small town. They had an elementary school but no church. They had a few businesses yet most of the population commuted elsewhere for work. The Chiswick Grange was the only building large enough to host community events, used for both voting and town meeting, yet the small population still managed to put this together.

Logan threaded her mittened hand through his elbow. "Well? What do you think?"

"It's magical." Her words came out on a sigh that turned into a puff of white in the cold night air. Fat snowflakes matted her eyelashes. Beside her was the most handsome man she knew, and, for at least a few months, he was her husband. She wanted to savor every moment of this, so when he asked if she'd like to go for a sleigh ride, her reply was an easy, "Of course."

A line of people waited ahead of them for their turn, including Jamie, Lauren, and their family. Prissy introduced her parents and sisters, and they stood chatting and stamping their feet to keep warm while the sleigh emptied and filled up again several times.

When it was their turn to climb aboard, Lulu and her parents sat on one bench seat while she, Logan and Muffy took the opposite side. "This is pretty," Lulu said, tucking the red and green plaid blanket across her lap.

Logan's eyebrows rose, and Prissy couldn't blame him. It was the first compliment from her older sister since she arrived in Ammonoosuc Falls.

"It almost makes the cold worth it," Muffy conceded.

"Stop, you, too," her mother admonished before snuggling against her father's side. "Don't spoil this perfect night."

Prissy couldn't agree more. Snow fell, lights sparkled, and people celebrated the season. When their marriage was over, and she was back in the Panhandle where cool air came from a vent in the ceiling and white was the color of clouds in the sky or waves foaming over the sand, she would remember this.

Too soon, the ride ended.

"What now?" her mother asked.

"I'd like to know the story behind that covered bridge," Lulu said.

"Come on," Logan waved toward the long red structure. "I'll show you."

They stopped beside the entrance to read the sign explaining how someone paid to move the bridge to the common from Littleton early in the twentieth century rather than see it demolished. "Since it was too big for any of the streams and not big enough for the river, they put it here in the middle of the town common," Logan added.

"How big is it?"

"It spans one hundred and fifty-six feet of grass. Or snow, depending on the season."

"What do they do with it?"

"It's kind of a tourist attraction. People come here and get their engagement photos taken. Especially in the fall when the leaves change color."

Prissy had arrived in Ammonoosuc Falls just after peak foliage, but it was pretty even then with the rust and orange colors. Painted red and gold, it would be a beautiful sight.

"Elementary kids come here on field trips to learn about engineering."

"Safer than standing over water, I guess," her mother said.

"Right. When they're older, they all come back for a group senior picture." He led them through the bridge, using the flashlight app on his phone to show them several years of senior photos hanging above the bridge windows. Prissy had traveled through the bridge daily when walking to the diner and back, as a kind of shortcut across the common, but they were too high up for her to have noticed with her short stature and her head down against the cold.

Now she scanned the images for his face. "Is there one of you?"

He pointed to a picture with seven young people, three boys and four girls. She recognized Chris in the middle of the bridge opening, wide enough to stand behind two girls and still touch the shoulders of the other two with his big hands. On either side of them, Jamie and Logan were propped against the bridge frame as if they were holding it up. "Too cool to smile for the camera?" she asked, noting their tough expressions.

He shrugged, then surprised her by explaining, "My front teeth were rotten. As soon as I got a job with benefits, I had them fixed."

"You have a beautiful smile," she whispered, hurting for the youthful Logan shuttled from house to house and having to pay for his own dental care.

"Come on." He led them through the bridge to the end facing Campbell's Country Store. "In the summer there are tables and chairs in here. People bring their lunch over from the deli, and on Friday nights they have pizza and play trivia games."

"That must be nice." Prissy's voice was unconsciously wistful because that was something she would enjoy but not be here to see.

Lulu gave her a sharp look, yet before she could say anything, a commotion on the common stole everyone's attention.

"Santa's here!" several children yelled.

Muffy grabbed Lulu's elbow. "Let's go see the big guy."

Santa circled the common on a John Deere tractor with a large evergreen, probably twelve feet tall, strapped to a trailer behind it. People clapped and cheered while he shouted, "Ho-ho-ho!"

"That is one big elf," her mother exclaimed.

Santa was indeed taller and wider than the average man, with paws for hands and giant-sized feet encased in shiny black boots. "Chris?" Prissy whispered to Logan, who nodded.

The tractor came to a stop. Santa stood up, one hand shielding his eyes while he made a show of peering into the crowd. "Where are my elves?"

Children rushed forward to volunteer.

"That's more like it. I can't put this tree up all by myself."

"And that's my cue." Logan tapped her nose with his finger. "Behave yourself while I'm gone." Voice dropped to a whisper, he added, "And before you say, 'arf, arf', it's not an order."

Prissy watched him go with equal parts longing and relief. The more playful he became, the harder it was for her to remember their agreement and protect her heart.

"That is one giant tree," her father noted.

"Hmm." Prissy was glad to have her family here for the holiday even if she had to sleep in the same bed with her husband and pretend they were a normal couple. "I can't wait to see it."

Chris, Logan, and Jamie put the tree up with help from a few volunteer firefighters and a ladder truck. When the evergreen was tied down with stakes, topped by a giant star and strung with lights, Santa asked the kids if they were ready for him to plug it in.

"Ready!" they chorused.

"Everyone better stand back. Don't want anyone going blind."

Logan returned to Prissy's side and took her hand. Muffy and Lulu rejoined them.

Chris made a show of connecting the lowest string of lights to an extension cord running out from the covered bridge.

A rainbow of colors illuminated the air.

"Oh, my stars," Prissy breathed.

Logan squeezed her hand. "Pretty, isn't it?"

A tame description. Muted by falling snow, the colored lights were magical, the brilliant star on top of the tree glowing high above the common.

"This is *so* worth standing out in the cold," Muffy admitted.

"Amen to that," their mother said.

Santa got back on his tractor and started the engine, circling the common toward the road leading to the Cote tree farm. When he passed their group, Muffy ran over and climbed up onto the seat beside him.

"Ho! Ho! Ho!" Santa waved, and they chugged away.

Logan didn't know what that was all about, but Muffy was home, asleep on the living room sofa when he came down in the middle of the night to retrieve Prissy's stocking. He didn't sneak into the room, it was his house after all, but when one of the floorboards creaked, she grumbled and rolled over.

"Sorry." He grabbed the red felt stocking from the mantle and turned to leave.

Muffy blinked and sat up. "Don't go."

Reluctantly, he stayed where he was, hoping she wasn't in the mood for a private conversation, though he'd rather talk to her than Lulu.

"My sister steals the covers," she said of that woman now. "She already had them all on her side of the bed when I got home, so I sacked out here. You don't mind?"

"No, but Prissy will probably be down at some point." He waved to the empty stockings hanging from the mantle. "I told her gifts under the tree were enough, but she put her foot down on this."

"She is stubborn." Muffy yawned and pulled the throw blanket tighter around her shoulders. "I don't suppose you have something else I could cover up with?"

Logan thought he'd seen Prissy put a blanket on the shelf above the coats in the foyer closet. He retrieved it and returned to the living room, handing it to Muffy. "This should help."

"Thanks. I don't know how you live with this cold."

"We're used to it," he shrugged. "Your sister doesn't complain about it." Not even at five in the morning when she walked across town without winter boots or a winter coat.

"What does she complain about?"

"Come again?"

"I mean, is there anything she *does* complain about?"

Logan thought about that for a moment, unable to come up with any examples.

"Right," Muffy said when he didn't reply. "She could be turning into an icicle, and you'd never hear a peep out of her."

"Why is that?" he wondered.

"She thinks she owes everyone for living. For being a burden when she was a kid because she had cancer, like it was her fault. She doesn't ask favors, and she insists on doing everything herself, on paying for everything herself or spending the least amount of money possible."

"Lulu said something like that," he remembered.

"She's the sweetest person in the world. Funny, too, but you probably know that."

He did, and he was reminded of her sense of humor when he stepped into the living room a few hours later and saw his stocking overflowing with fresh cut flowers.

"I didn't know what you liked," she grinned from where she was curled up in an easy chair. "So, I told them to give me three dozen and make sure you got one of everything."

"How thoughtful of you."

Her cheeks pinkened, more so when he leaned down and brushed her lips in greeting, for the benefit of her parents who sat on the sofa and her sisters who were coming down the stairs.

"Merry Christmas." He handed her the stocking he had hidden behind his back, red and green grapes spilling out of the top of it.

Prissy squealed with laughter.

Logan felt something stir inside his chest at her reaction.

"You need to get your stocking," Prissy urged, "so we can open them together."

Taking his from the mantle, he returned to sit on the arm of Prissy's chair. He pulled the flowers out and laid them on the coffee table. "This is heavy," he noted, wondering what was inside and perplexed when he found six rolls of pennies. He held one up and looked to her for explanation.

"I've been saving them for you, for the savings account." Her eyes lit with mischief. "Because you say every penny counts."

Logan chuckled at her explanation. "Your turn."

She wrinkled her pert little nose and withdrew the grapes from her stocking, then removed two dark plastic bags from the bottom. "What are they?"

"Scarves." He hadn't known she wore them to cover surgical reminders on her neck, but he had noticed that she wore them a lot and thought she could use some new patterns.

Prissy opened the bags and fingered the colored fabrics inside. "I love them. Thank you."

Just because she got excited over her stocking didn't mean she'd like her other gifts. He worried a little about that, telling himself it was because her parents and sisters were sharing the tree with them, but a small part of him acknowledged a desire to make her happy.

Her parents gave him a book written by a famous chef he admired, making his, "Thank you," easy and sincere. From Lulu he got a framed photo of Prissy as a little girl, all big brown eyes beneath silky blond bangs, tan limbs and a happy smile. She was sitting on a tricycle decorated with red, white and blue streamers, a cocker spaniel puppy at her side wearing a similarly colored ribbon around its neck. "You were cute," he said, meaning it, wondering what it must have been like to have such a carefree childhood, determined to give his niece or nephew the same.

"Me next." Muffy handed him a package which turned out to be an engine block heater. "Because it's freezing here. I don't know how you stand it, big brother."

"He's not your brother," Lulu corrected.

"Of course he is. He married my sister."

"Would you please tell her the difference?" she begged her parents.

That plea fell on deaf ears. Somewhere between their arrival and last night's dinner, they had apparently decided to accept him, so they refused to give Lulu the backup she wanted.

"My turn," Prissy interjected, passing a rectangular box to Logan. It was wrapped in blue and silver paper and a blue ribbon stretched across the corners.

Inside he found a high-quality leather belt. "To replace the one I stole," she explained.

"So you admit you stole it?" When she blushed at his teasing, he took pity on her and passed her a gift. "This one is from me."

She laughed on seeing what was inside, drawing out the thin braided belt with a tortoiseshell buckle. "Just my style. Thank you."

"Wait, there's more." Muffy drew the last two gifts out from under the tree. "One for each of you." She looked at the tags. "From each of you."

Prissy went first, but when the gift was unwrapped, she stared at it without speaking.

Had he picked the wrong style? The wrong color? "If you don't like it, you can take it back and get something else."

She shook her head mutely, pulling the dress from the box and standing to shake it out and hold it against her body as if posing before a mirror.

"Oh, Prissy," Muffy breathed, "that is *so* you."

That's what Logan had thought when he saw it in the store. A soft olive green, the sweater dress had a high mock neck and a layer of knit wrapped around the front from the side seams, tied with a bow in the middle of the chest like a bikini top, giving the dress shape and definition.

Prissy still hadn't said anything. Uncertain of her reaction, he explained, "I thought you could wear it for the housewarming party."

"You might not be as clueless as you seem," Lulu remarked.

Prissy smoothed a hand over the soft fabric. "Don't talk to my husband that way." When she finally looked at him, her doe brown eyes shone. "I love it."

"Now let's see what you got him."

Logan didn't understand her gift. It was a weird plastic hat, with two mirrors extending up from the temples, facing backward.

"What in the world?" her mother took it from him and turned it over, looked at it from different angles then shrugged helplessly and passed it to her husband.

Prissy was suspiciously red in the face now. "Care to explain?" Logan asked.

"You seem to have eyes in the back of your head. If you wear this, you really will."

"Come again?"

If possible, her blush deepened. "You always catch me when I stick my tongue out."

"Priscilla Daphne Nicole Schermerhorn!" her mother gasped, looking horrified. "I know I taught you better manners than that."

Logan couldn't help but laugh. Pulling Prissy close, he said, "You got me this time."

Instead of replying, she turned her face and their lips brushed accidentally. He knew it wasn't intentional because her eyes went wide, but with her family watching, he had no choice but to play along.

He kissed her. Not a long, deep kiss, but more than a peck. Tender enough that maybe even Lulu would be convinced they had a real marriage. Pulling back slowly with a reluctance that was not entirely faked, he said, "Thank you."

"There's more."

"Oh?" He looked at the box in his hand and noticed a layer of brown paper covering a rectangular item. Removing it from the box, he peeled back the paper to reveal a framed photograph that made his heart turn over.

"What is it?" "Show us."

Logan turned the picture around for her family to see.

"Is it this house?" Muffy asked.

He nodded. A few things had changed since the black and white photo was taken. The maple trees were still saplings then, the garage and side porch hadn't yet been added. He let them admire it for a few moments before turning it around and taking a closer look. That's when he noticed a woman and two children sitting on the front lawn.

"Who are the people?"

Prissy leaned closer to him, pointing to the woman. "That's Cora Dunlap."

Logan had never seen a photo of her when she was young.

"The girl is your grandmother. The baby is Ivy's mother. I didn't know that's who they were until I showed it to her."

"Where did you get it?"

"You know that shop in Lisbon where we got the clock? The one you didn't think had anything worth looking at?"

He might have walked right by it and never known. Yet Prissy had found this treasure there and brought it home for him. Her thoughtfulness amazed him.

This time he was the one who couldn't speak.

Chapter Fourteen

Prissy assumed they would lounge around until lunchtime, but as soon as they had picked up the wrapping paper, Logan announced he had to go out for a while.

"Would you like to come with me?"

Conscious of her family watching, she nodded as if she knew where they were going. "You're all welcome to join us," he told them.

"Sounds like a mystery." "Sure, why not?" "Girls, you can ride with us."

Prissy peppered him with questions on the drive, but he wouldn't tell her anything. Even when he turned onto the road leading to A Notch Above, which she knew was closed for the holiday, he wouldn't explain.

There were a few cars in the employee parking lot. Logan pulled in beside them and came around to open her door. "Will you tell me now?"

He waited for her family to join them, grinned and said, "Follow me."

Inside, Ricky was using a commercial mixer to mash a huge pot of boiled potatoes. Chris dribbled maple glaze over a pan of roasted butternut squash. Black marker in hand, Ivy wrote names and addresses on take-out container boxes.

Logan spread his arms wide to encompass the busy kitchen. "Welcome to Santa's workshop. We make Christmas meals for shut-ins and people who live alone and deliver them before lunchtime."

Prissy's heart rolled over in her chest. This was the Logan the townspeople knew. A grateful, generous man. One who she had tried but couldn't possibly protect herself against.

The back door slamming open gave her a moment to regain control. Matthew stepped into the room with four cardboard boxes, followed by Shelly carrying four more. "Pie's here!"

That day marked a change in their relationship. He sought her opinion more often. His comments were no longer objectionable. They talked in bed at night before falling asleep.

Like a couple in the first stages of dating, they were getting to know one another. What started out as necessary research now seemed like genuine curiosity.

Birthday? April 10. Age? Twenty-four.

Favorite season? Spring.

"Why is that?"

"Because the flowers bloom. Everywhere."

Favorite movie?

"Purple Hearts."

"Never heard of it."

She wasn't about to tell him it was a tale of two people marrying for convenience, so she settled for, "It's a love story."

"Figures."

Favorite music? Pop.

Favorite food? Banana pudding.

"Eww! Really?"

She slapped his arm and accused him of being a copycat.

Favorite color?

"Pink." She snuggled into the pillow and yawned. "You probably figured that one out, since the rock on my finger is a pink one." A ring she secretly cherished because it showed he knew her tastes.

"Go to sleep, Prissy. We've got a big day tomorrow."

Good advice, though a sound night's sleep didn't keep her from being a nervous wreck while waiting for their first guests to arrive the next evening.

It was one thing to insist they host this party, but it was another to play the role of happy wife to a man who said he didn't want her yet seemed to suddenly enjoy her company. How many times over the last few days had he reached for her hand? How many times had he brushed hair off her cheek or swooped in for an unexpected kiss? She understood the need to make it look real for her family, but it was getting harder for Prissy to remember that none of this was.

She had expected things to get easier after Christmas, because the diner reopened and she went back to work, but she was wrong.

She no longer had any alone time. At work, someone inevitably asked how her first holiday with her husband was and she pretended to be a happy newlywed. At home, the charade continued for her family.

Tonight would be more of the same. She was afraid she would either crack and admit their deception or throw herself at Logan and beg him to make their marriage real.

Instead of doing either of those things, she donned her new sweater dress, pasted a smile on her face, and welcomed friends and acquaintances to their home. She took care of coats. She helped the restaurant staff with drinks and hors d'oeuvres. She gave tours to guests and thanked them graciously for the gifts they were told not to bring but had anyway.

When Logan put his arm around her shoulders, she leaned into his side and gazed lovingly into his blue eyes.

It wasn't hard. In fact, it was hard not to.

Sometime during the party, she finally admitted what she had been hiding from herself for days; she was in love with her husband.

"Are you okay?" he whispered at her ear.

Prissy nodded, unable to reply.

"You look shell shocked. Did someone say something to upset you?

"No." Giving herself a mental shake, she added, "Probably just nerves."

"You've got nothing to worry about. Just look around you."

Gil was speaking with Martin and Kathy. Ivy, Lauren, and her sisters were at the breakfast table together with little Chris in a baby carrier between them. Big Chris carried Emmy around the room on his shoulder so she could bat at the Christmas decorations hanging from the ceiling. Ricky and Matthew played a video game in the nook behind the staircase. Her parents and Shelly were in the formal dining room with the town clerk. Thalia and Darla sat in the living room with their dates. Everyone appeared to be having a good time.

Others came and went over the next three hours, and by the time she closed the door on the last guest, Prissy was drooping.

"You should go to bed," Logan told her.

"I've got picking up to do."

"No, you don't. My staff will take care of the food and drink, and I'll take care of anything else." He gently nudged her shoulder. "You've been up since five. Go."

Sun coming in through the bedroom window woke her the next morning and she bolted upright. What time was it? The clock on the nightstand showed ten past seven. She never overslept!

Scrambling free of bedding, she pulled on a turtleneck and leggings and rushed out of the room, almost colliding with Logan in the hallway.

"I thought I heard you moving about." He pressed a steaming mug of coffee into her hands. "Sleep well?"

"Like the dead," she admitted, then almost squealed, "My family is leaving in an hour!"

He smiled, and she caught her breath, remembering a time when she had wondered if that expression would ever be for her. "Guess we'd better get down there, then."

An hour later they stood on the front steps, waving to the departing Schermerhorns.

Muffy rolled the back window down to add one more, "Love you!"

"Love you more than rainbows!" Prissy shouted back, biting her lip when a few tears slipped over her lashes and rolled down her cheeks. If she didn't scrub them away, maybe Logan wouldn't notice.

She should have known better. After all, this was the man with proverbial eyes in the back of his head.

"It's not goodbye," he said, squeezing her shoulder lightly. "It's just goodbye for now."

"I know." She scrubbed her face with both hands. "I'm just being silly."

"It's okay. You're a close family. It's normal to miss them."

"Thanks."

Recovering when the car was out of sight and hearing distance, Prissy turned to go inside. She had only taken one step when his next words brought her to a standstill.

"When we divorce, I'll tell everyone it's because you missed your family and wanted to go home to Florida."

Her heart stopped beating. Not literally, but she froze and held her breath against the agonizing pain of his words.

He wasn't done yet. "That way people won't think it's your fault. I'll say I couldn't go with you because of the restaurant, and the baby."

If she listened to one more word, she'd crumple to the ground in agony. "I have to go."

"What I meant—"

She opened the door and hurried into the house.

Logan followed her to the kitchen. "Prissy—"

"I promised Gil I'd stop by and pick up some flowers," she interrupted, "and I might as well go now. We may do some shopping, too. Do you need anything while I'm out?"

"Can we talk about this?"

She grabbed her coat from the stand beside the kitchen door and threw a tight smile over her shoulder at him, not making eye contact. "Sorry, I'll be late," she lied, and left before he could say anything else.

Logan stood at the kitchen door and watched her drive away.

Why had he said those things to her?

Was it self-preservation? Was it because they had a temporary arrangement, and he couldn't let himself get too close? Women left him. His mother. His aunt. His great grandmother.

He and Prissy had been building toward something over the holiday season.

Her soft breathing lulled him to sleep at night, her small body curled up next to his brought comfort he had never known.

She wasn't a flaky girl after an easy life or ten seconds of fame. She was smart, funny, and a hard worker. Ricky was right when he said she was nice to everyone. Last night she made each guest welcome and comfortable, even the nasty Darla and her boyfriend. Logan had watched her circulate among the partygoers and help the caterers until he wanted to scoop her off her feet and force her to sit down and take a break.

He hadn't wanted or asked for a wife, but he never meant to hurt her.

Grabbing his jacket and truck keys, he took off after her.

A few miles away, the parking lot at Gil's funeral home was empty. He drove around back and found the same.

Her car wasn't at the diner. Or on the common.

Frustrated, but hoping she might have returned home while he was out, he retraced his route and almost missed her.

She was parked on the logging road where they had gone to get to know one another and make sure their stories were straight. Her head rested on the car steering wheel, turned away from him, and she didn't seem to have heard him pull in because when he got out of the truck and shut the door, she jerked upright in her seat.

She didn't have time to hide her tears before he got in on the passenger side.

"I'm sorry," he said before she could pre-empt him. "I thought I was offering you something that would make you happy."

She stared mutely at him.

Reaching out with one hand, slowly so as not to startle her, he brushed tears from her cheek. "I didn't mean to make you cry."

When she still said nothing, he reached across the console and pulled her close. "Can you tell me why?"

She shook her head and burrowed her face against his shoulder.

"Is there anything I can do to make it better?"

She stilled, then slowly pushed away from him. Her soft brown eyes were clear, though still wet, her voice steady when she said, "Kiss me."

Wondering if he was making the biggest mistake of their short-term marriage, he nonetheless took her face in his hands and leaned down to kiss her. Once. Twice. The third time she opened her mouth, and he couldn't resist the invitation.

The kiss was warm, and soft, a welcome wrapped up in forgiveness.

When they broke apart, she traced the outline of his mouth with one finger.

"Thank you," she whispered.

Logan didn't know what to say to that.

Prissy relaxed back into her seat. "I really did tell Gil I'd be over."

"There's no car in his parking lot."

When she raised her eyebrows in question, he explained, "I went there looking for you."

"His car interior is being detailed. He says he gets it done on December 31, every year, so he can start the new year fresh."

"Hmm."

"So, I guess I'd better get going." She pulled her seat belt on and clicked the buckle into place. "Thanks again, Logan. For checking on me."

He nodded, opened the passenger door and stepped out. "I've got to go into work early."

"Lots of New Year's Eve revelers?"

"Yeah."

"I'll see you tonight, then."

He closed the door and rapped once on the hood before circling the car and getting into his truck. He let her pull out first but when she turned in the direction of Gil's funeral home, he went the other way, hitting speed dial on his phone as he drove.

"Logan," Ivy's crisp voice answered.

"Are you doing anything today?"

"Hanging out with Prince, watching Rudolph's Shiny New Year."

"I was hoping you could come by the restaurant later."

"You want me to get out of my pajamas on one of the few days I take off from work, go out into the cold and drive all the way up to Ammonoosuc Falls?" She groaned as if he was asking the world of her.

"I need to talk to you."

"About?"

He almost choked on the words, "Relationship stuff," not because it bothered him to admit he needed her advice, but because she'd have a field day with that admission.

"Hallelujah! At last. Wait a minute. This better be about Prissy?"

"Yeah."

"I'm still not coming up there for you, but I'm setting up my video chat right now."

"No rush. I'm in the truck, still five minutes from the house."

"See you in ten minutes, then. I've got to make a pot of coffee before I tackle this."

"You got it."

Ivy had said ten minutes, but if she wasn't early to a meeting, she considered herself late. Sure enough, a chime on his computer announced an incoming call sixty seconds before she was expected and just as he took a seat at his dining room table.

"Hope you like the pajamas," she said by way of greeting.

"Cute. If you were a thirteen-year-old, that is."

"Hey, don't knock it." Her fuzzy red top had reindeer dancing across the chest and her white flannel pants were decorated with the same. She wore red slipper socks with big white pom-poms on the top that bounced as she rearranged herself in one corner of her sofa.

None but her closest friends got to see her like this.

"You have coffee?"

"Of course." She lifted a giant mug half the size of her face and took a big swallow. She loved caffeine and argued that no good negotiation happened without it.

Prince leaped up onto the sofa, resting his silky head in her lap. "Hey, buddy," Logan greeted. The dog lifted his head slightly and wagged his tail once.

"So, tell me, before we begin, am I here as a lawyer, or as a friend?"

Ivy never did waste time.

Logan adjusted his laptop screen against a glare of sunlight coming in through the window behind him and got right to it. "I upset Prissy this morning."

"Oh?"

"I wanted to change the terms of our agreement."

"How so?"

"I said that when we divorce, I'll tell people she was homesick for her family, and I couldn't move to Florida because of the restaurant."

Ivy narrowed her eyes above the rim of her coffee cup. He'd like to think it was from the steam, but he knew better, and it put him on the defensive. "Anyone who saw her with them will believe it."

Her expression didn't change.

"That way neither one of us will look like the 'bad guy' in this."

"That's debatable."

"Come again?"

"Never mind. You said she was upset by it?"

An understatement. But since Ivy wasn't exactly offering sympathy or advice, he wasn't going to share the details of Prissy's reaction. Instead, he came to a sudden decision. "I still want to change the terms of the agreement."

"She would have to *agree* too, you know; that's the root of the word."

"Okay, then not the agreement we signed, but I want to write a will."

Ivy put her coffee down and shook her head slowly from side to side. "I'm having a hard time following here."

"I'll need a will for the baby, anyway." His chest caved in at the thought of having, and leaving, a child before it reached adulthood. "I want a will that says if anything happens to me before our marriage ends, Prissy gets the whole check from the reality show."

"That's doable."

Logan relaxed in his seat.

"But you didn't take me away from Rudolph for a will. You said this was about relationship advice."

How to explain? He bounced his leg up and down, realized he was doing it, and stopped. He ran a hand down the back of his neck. Finally, he admitted, "I like her."

"Of course you do."

"Come again?"

"What's not to like? Everyone who meets her feels the same way."

"Not Chris."

"Even Chris is coming around."

He had noticed his friend no longer made snarky comments about her.

"Give her a chance."

Logan nodded, though he wasn't sure what her new role would be. No longer an unwanted legal obligation, but more than just a temporary house mate. "Okay. Thanks, Ivy."

Chapter Fifteen

Gil ushered Prissy into an office next to the main reception area. "This is where I meet with families," he explained.

Paneled curtains on the French doors matched two chintz sofas on either side of a coffee table, a dried flower arrangement decorating the top of that polished surface and a leather-bound book on either side of that bouquet. Prissy admired the warmth of the décor. "It's nice."

"I try to make it as comfortable for them as possible. Drinks," he waved to a small refrigerator against the wall with a coffee service on top of it. "Sample programs." He sat on a sofa and motioned for her to join him, then opened one of the leather-bound books to show her printed copies of past services. "We have a pianist that we contract with in case they want music. We can stream it, too, but a lot of people prefer it live." He smiled ruefully. "I still say we, but I guess it's just me now."

Prissy scanned the pages in the book, poetry, collections of memories, and artwork. "How long have you been doing this?"

"Years. Since I came home from college. My father ran the business before me, but neither of my brothers were interested in it. They moved away."

"And what will you do when you retire?"

"I don't know." He sighed, fatigue and worry settling wrinkling his brow. "I'd rather not see the business close, but there aren't many people interested in running a funeral home these days. I'm not sure I could even find a buyer, and if I did, I'd have to move out of my house."

Prissy came to the end of the book and handed it back to him. "Maybe you could arrange for life tenancy."

"Maybe," he agreed, slapping his knees and rising to his feet. "Do you want to see the rest of the place before we go shopping?"

"Yes, please."

Anyone else might have pretended an interest in the funeral home, but Prissy loved science and was genuinely curious. Gil led her through the chapel, visitation rooms and offices, then into the prep room.

"You're not squeamish?" he asked before opening that door.

"No." At his raised eyebrows, she explained, "Blood and needles were part of my childhood."

"You were sick?"

Nodding, she rolled down the turtleneck of her sweater and revealed her scars. "Throat cancer. Between surgery, follow-up treatments and appointments, I spent a lot of time in hospitals." That was what first inspired her to go into medicine and, though she had decided against a career in that field, anything to do with the human body was still fascinating to her.

There were no bodies in the prep room. The large, cool space was spotless. Gil showed her the embalming equipment and refrigeration units, explained how the blood was disposed of since there was no municipal sewage system in Ammonoosuc Falls, and gave her a quick history lesson on how funeral homes had changed over the years.

"You said you aren't squeamish," he said when they returned to the reception area at the front of the building, "but it's almost lunch time. Will you be able to eat?"

"Yes." At his dubious look, she insisted, "I'm fine, really. There's nothing gross to me about what you do. Every person deserves to be cared for when they die. You treat them with respect, and I can tell you do your best to honor the family's wishes. That's a special thing."

Gil's wrinkles split and rearranged themselves into a smile.

"It must be a privilege to take care of someone's loved one for the last time."

"It is. That's exactly what it is."

"Thank you for showing me. Now, didn't you say something about lunch?"

They had sandwiches at Campbell's Country Store before leaving for Littleton where Prissy bought two white shirts for work, long-sleeved and high necked, a pair of corduroy pants, and two sweaters. They spent half an hour perusing the candy selection at Chutter's, a store credited by the Guinness Book of World Records for having the longest continuous candy counter in the world, and out on the sidewalk, Gil held their bags of treats while Prissy tipped a busker playing Christmas carols on a ukelele.

It was a fun, carefree day, and she didn't think about that morning, or Logan, or the hourglass leaking sand toward the end of their marriage.

It all came back as soon as she parked by the kitchen door.

The house was empty. After the last few days with her parents and sisters visiting, and Logan spending time with her, she didn't want to step inside and hear her footsteps echo on the hardwood floors.

"This will never do," she scolded herself. The man hadn't asked for this marriage, and he had been clear from the beginning about how it would end. She was the fool who imagined it as something more. She had to own that heartache and the responsibility for it now.

Her phone dinged. Pulling it from her crossbody bag, she saw a message from her parents that everyone had arrived home safely. She sent back a happy face and a few hearts, grabbed her flowers and purchases from the passenger seat, and went inside.

Logan had left the outside light on. In the house, she used her phone to guide her through the main floor and up the stairs because despite her little pep talk in the car, she wasn't ready to turn on the lights and face the emptiness right now.

She moved her things into the bedroom her sisters had shared. It was inevitable, practical, and kept her busy. Yet when she crawled beneath the covers, she yearned for the warmth of Logan's body beside her. Her ears listened for his breathing. Her heart ached without him. She had once thought the stress of her financial burdens would kill her. That was nothing compared to this.

PRISSY'S CAR WINDOWS were glazed with ice when Logan got home but the house was dark. Assuming she was already asleep, he turned off the outside light, tiptoed through the house and up the stairs.

His bed was empty.

A quick inspection showed her side of the closet barren, the dresser drawers she had been using now cleaned out.

He checked the little room where he sometimes heard her sewing, in case she fell asleep over her machine, flicked on the light switch, and came to a standstill.

Muted lamps cast a soft glow over what was now a woodland nursery. Curtains decorated with baby animals framed the closet aperture, a mobile of woodland creatures dangling above the bassinette within. A baby quilt, valance over the single window, and padded cushion on a white rocking chair in the corner were all made of the same material, with foxes and bunnies and squirrels prancing through the forest.

A fox kit from the fabric had been lacquered to the chair's headrest. Beside it a small white dresser had been turned into a changing table with a matching padded cover.

This had taken some time. Imagination. Caring. Logan didn't know what to think.

Even allowing for Prissy's love of pretty things and comfortable surroundings, this was a lot. Why would she do this for a child she'd hardly know? The baby wasn't due for another five weeks. They had been married now for seven. He'd done a lot of reading since he found out about Dummer's child, and at twelve weeks old the baby might recognize her but then she'd be gone, and he or she would never remember Prissy or her efforts to make this room into a nursery.

Disturbed, he turned off the lights and quietly closed the door.

He found her sleeping in the room her sisters had shared. Light from the hall outlined her small frame curled beneath the covers. Her hair fanned out across the pillow and her hands were folded beneath her cheek like a small child.

Her phone was charging on the nightstand. She had laid out her work clothes on the bench at the foot of the bed and her combat boots were tucked neatly beneath it. He stood and listened to her breathing for a few minutes, his insides churning with a mix of emotions he wasn't sure he could separate or understand.

Eventually he closed this door, too, and retreated down the hall.

After sharing a bedroom with her for almost two months, the space felt empty.

How had she got under his skin this much in such a short amount of time? What did she want from him? What did the nursery mean? And why had she been crying this morning?

As if he had broadcast those questions to the universe at large to answer, his phone buzzed. A number he didn't recognize flashed across the screen. He picked up, anyway, because it was one thirty in the morning so the call could be important.

"Hello?"

"Happy New Year, brother," Muffy sang out gaily. "Do you miss me?"

"Like a toothache," he grinned. Prissy's little sister was sweet like one but almost as aggravating.

"Aww, the things you say."

"What are you doing awake at this hour?"

"Jet lag."

"We live in the same time zone."

"Okay, call it whatever you want. I couldn't sleep. Maybe I got used to your cold weather and it's too warm here."

"That's hard to believe."

Her carefree laugh agreed with him. "Anyway, I just called to wish you a good start to the year. I've got to call Chris next."

That surprised him. "You and Chris?" he wondered aloud.

"That's a hard no."

Then why did she ride off with him on Christmas Eve? And why was she calling him now? In answer to those unspoken questions, she said, "I asked to see the cabin Prissy stayed in. He's going to rent it to a friend of mine for a few months. I have lots of friends, you know."

He didn't doubt it.

"And now Chris is one of them."

"Okay." Logan was tempted to hold his hands up and surrender. "I get it."

"Good. I know Prissy will be sleeping, but please tell her I love her."

"Will do."

"Love you too, big brother."

Logan hadn't heard anyone say that to him since Dummer was ten or eleven years old. Muffy's insistence that he was one of the family both warmed and scared him. Warmed, because it made him feel wanted, scared, because it would end when he and Prissy divorced so he didn't want to get used to it.

"It's okay if you don't say it back yet. I'll grow on you."

"Uh-huh." Just like her sister. "Have a good night, Mary Margaret."

"Toodle Loo."

He dropped the phone onto his bed and went into the bathroom to clean up, but it was buzzing again when he came out. "Muffy," he groaned into the device, "I would like to get some sleep tonight."

"You can live without a few more minutes of beauty rest," came Ada's sharp reply. Maybe this was a tag team event. What did that make him. Opponent? Referee? Prize?

"You are still there, right?"

Logan dropped down onto the edge of his bed. "I'm here."

"I called to say thank you for this week."

"Okay." He didn't take that comment at face value.

"You're supposed to say, 'you're welcome' when someone says that."

"Yes, ma'am," he replied sarcastically, "you're welcome. What did you really call for?"

"You get smarter every time I talk to you."

"I'm going to hang up now."

"Don't."

"Give me one good reason not to."

"Prissy."

"What about her?"

"I don't know what the deal between you two is, but I know you made one."

He neither confirmed nor denied her statement.

"I've watched some of that reality show online. Previews, since it hasn't aired yet. You aren't a member of the cast."

"I never said I was."

"And I don't believe Prissy's story about love at first sight for a minute."

"Thanks for the compliment."

"This isn't about you."

"Then you should get to the point so I can get some sleep before the sun comes up."

"Break her heart and I'll bust your acorns."

Coming from anyone else, Logan might have laughed, but he knew she meant it. Prissy was her little sister. She would protect her with everything she had, so he ignored the insult to his male anatomy and the threat to those body parts, offering what reassurance he could. "I don't plan to hurt her."

"Spoken like a man who isn't even aware that he could."

"Goodnight, Ada Louella Louise."

Logan put his phone on mute and turned it upside down on the nightstand.

He needed that quiet. Over the next few days, he realized he needed the space Prissy had put between them just as much. Having her family here had given him a false sense of belonging, and he couldn't afford to get attached to people who were temporary.

Prissy had done a good job at the party, at decorating the house and the nursery, but she wouldn't stay. She would leave like the other women in his life.

The best way to prepare himself for that eventuality was to get used to it now.

Chapter Sixteen

They reverted to their pre-holiday routine. Prissy left before him in the morning, he was gone to the restaurant before she came home in the afternoon. Occasionally their paths crossed, but they both managed to avoid spending that time together.

He missed her. More than he had expected to, which had him questioning his actions, his feelings, and the fast-approaching end to their marriage. Could he live like this for the next four months, occupying the same space yet hardly interacting? Yes. He had done it before. Did he want to? No. He just wasn't sure how to breach the gap between them.

Cherilyn took care of that for them.

He was prepping for dinner service on a snowy Thursday afternoon in January when she called to say she was in labor and on her way to the hospital.

Logan didn't know what he said to his staff. He didn't remember calling his friends or getting in his truck and leaving A Notch Above. When he found himself standing inside the door of the Chiswick Diner, he had no memory of driving there.

Prissy took one look at hm and rushed right over. "What's wrong?"

He opened his mouth to reply, but nothing came out. Unexpected tears spurted into his eyes and a lump the size of a softball seemed lodged in his throat.

Prissy gripped his forearm, her brown eyes wide with concern. "Logan? Are you okay?"

He shook his head. His leg bounced. It took a monumental effort to breathe, but he finally managed to say, "Cherilyn's in labor."

"Isn't this early?"

He ran a hand through his hair and gripped the nape of his neck. "Two weeks. They say it's not unusual, but I don't know. I've got to get down there,to Portsmouth."

"Do you want me to come with you?"

"What?" *Yes.* "No, you're still working. I just came to let you know what's happening."

"You're driving yourself?"

"What?" He jangled the truck keys in his hand, shifted his weight from one foot to the other, and glanced at the door. "I need to go."

"Wait!" Prissy clutched his elbow before he could turn away. "Do you have a place to stay tonight? Do you have the baby's car seat with you?"

He stared at her, trying to understand what she was asking but coming up with nothing.

"Babies are usually released the day after they're born," she explained. "Are you going to stay the night and bring the baby home tomorrow?"

Logan didn't have time for these questions. "I've got to go."

"Let me ask Shelly if I can go with you. That way I can drive while you worry."

"What makes you think I'm worried?"

Prissy's gaze went soft. "Who wouldn't be?"

The ride to Portsmouth was a nightmare of snow, sleet, and freezing rain mixed with heavy fog, taking a full hour longer than usual.

By the time he was scrubbed and draped in protective gear, he was almost out of his mind with worry. Finding Cherilyn lying back in a comfortable chair, having her hair braided by an attending nurse was the last thing he expected.

On the phone she had made the birth seem imminent.

"You're okay," he stated the obvious. He didn't know if he should collapse from relief or throttle the girl for scaring years off his life.

"This must be the uncle," the nurse observed, finishing the braid. She stepped away from Cherilyn and he moved closer.

"Hi, Logan."

That breezy greeting did nothing to calm his nerves. He had just driven through an insane storm to get here. Correction: Prissy had driven through it, and by the looks of things they could have taken their time.

"What's going on?" he asked when he was certain he had himself under control.

"Nothing at the moment." She settled back into the pillow, long golden braid draped over her shoulder. "The labor stopped. Again."

"What does that mean?"

"They're going to do a C-section. We were just waiting for you to get here."

Relief flooded him, immediately followed by renewed concern. "Is that normal? I mean, is everything okay?"

"It will be." She stretched her arms out to him, inviting him in for a hug, but when he closed the gap between them, she gripped his shoulders tight and whispered, "Whatever you do, do *not* let my parents have this child."

He pulled back a few inches and she smiled serenely, putting on a show for the nurse.

Behind them, the door opened and a woman wearing a pretty sweater and casual slacks walked in. "Hello, I'm Doctor Frenkiewich. Are we ready to roll now that the gang's all here?"

An hour later he cradled his nephew in his arms. A precious, perfect baby with a wisp of light brown hair on his soft, tiny head and ten miniscule fingernails on his tiny, crimped fingers. Logan had counted each one.

"Does he look like his father?" Cherilyn whispered, clearing her throat before adding, "I've never seen a baby picture of him, so I can't tell."

Logan couldn't reply, joy and sorrow warring in his chest and strangling his vocal chords. This baby was everything to him, the family he never had, the future his little brother should have had. Yet he knew, better than most, how quickly things could change.

"Are you sure?" he asked Cherilyn.

"He's yours." Tears glistened in her eyes, but her voice was steady, and her expression was resolute. "It's what Dummer would have wanted."

The nurse pretended not to hear them, organizing items on a cabinet that probably didn't need organizing. Logan appreciated her discretion and this peaceful moment, shattered when Cherilyn's parents came into the room, the doctor behind them.

They asked a lot of questions. About how their daughter was doing, and how soon she would be able to go home, only peeking at the baby in his arms but not asking to hold him until the doctor and nurse exchanged a look of surprise.

Unfortunately, Cherilyn's mother saw it, and she went from disinterested to cooing over the baby like he was the sweetest little thing she'd ever seen.

"Will the two of you have a role in his life?" the nurse asked, and Logan wished she had kept silent because the two-word reply, "Oh, absolutely," changed everything.

"That's good. A child needs all the love and support it can get."

The baby wheezed. His little chest rose, and he wheezed again when it fell.

"We need to clear the room," the nurse said, her tone alerting him that something was wrong even if he hadn't already sensed it.

Within minutes the baby was whisked away. Suspected RSV, the doctor said, but Logan couldn't hear or process her words. She must have realized that, because she finally gripped his shoulder and said, "Mr. Shaw? Is there anyone here with you?"

Logan shook himself free of his paralysis and croaked, "My wife is in the waiting area."

The doctor escorted him there to find Prissy curled up in a chair, sound asleep. She woke when the door swished closed behind them, coming to her feet as soon as she saw his face. "What is it? What's wrong?"

"You must be Mrs. Shaw," the doctor said with a reassuring smile that did nothing to ease Logan's mind. "Please, have a seat."

Prissy fell back into her chair and Logan dropped into the one beside her. The doctor pulled a third chair away from the wall and sat in front of them. "Have you ever heard of RSV?"

"I have some experience with it," Prissy said, surprising Logan. "I went to med school for two years," she explained. "Before that I worked in the pediatric trauma center at a hospital in Pensacola. Does the baby have RSV?"

"We're running some tests on him now."

"A boy?" Prissy offered Logan a smile of congratulations.

In all his fear, he had forgotten to tell her. He had also forgotten that he wasn't alone, and that the person he completely abandoned on entering this building was probably the one most qualified to help him through this.

"As soon as I know more, I'll be out to see you," the doctor said, rising and replacing her chair against the wall. "I assume we have your cell phone number?"

Logan nodded.

"It shouldn't be long."

The door swished closed on her departure and the room fell silent. Prissy reached out and stroked his clenched fist. He unfolded his fingers, and when she would have withdrawn her hand, he surprised them both by clutching it.

"Logan?"

"I'm sorry," he exhaled.

"For what?"

"For yelling at you on the way down. For leaving you here on your own."

"It's okay."

"No, not really." She had never driven in weather like that before. She must have been terrified, yet he barked directions at her then spent the rest of his time glued to his cellphone so he wouldn't miss any incoming messages.

"You had more important things on your mind."

"Stop making excuses for me, Prissy."

"Come again?"

He smiled tiredly. "That's my line."

"I stole it."

"Like my belt. Maybe I should start a list."

"Tell me about your son."

He opened his mouth to reply only to close it again. Unexpected tears filled his eyes and clogged his throat. He had to swallow them down before he could speak. "He's perfect."

"Of course he is. Does he look like Dummer?"

"I honestly have no idea who he looks like."

"Congratulations, Logan." She unzipped her bag and withdrew a cellophane wrapped cigar, tied with a blue ribbon, the words, "It's a boy!" written in blue script along the side.

Accepting the gift, he dropped his head and closed his eyes.

Small arms surrounded his heaving shoulders. She pulled him to her chest and stroked his hair. As a child, he had yearned for a woman to hold him like this, to reassure him everything would be okay. He knew that outcome was anything but certain, yet he lost himself in her embrace until the storm passed.

"Do you have a name for him?" she asked, her voice as soft as her touch.

"Bodie."

"That's nice." Prissy moved back to her chair. "Does it have any special meaning?"

"No," he shrugged. "I just liked it. But his full name will be Bodie Dunlap Shaw."

The door swished open. Logan tensed on seeing the doctor, his joy at being a father, and having someone of his own in this world, once again marred by worry for the baby's health. He came to his feet, too nervous to sit and wait for what she had to say. Beside him, Prissy rose and took his hand.

"Mr. and Mrs. Shaw. The test results show your baby has RSV, but he's exactly where he needs to be right now. We'll keep him here, make sure he gets plenty of fluids, oxygen if he needs it, and if everything goes well, we'll send him home with you in a few days. How does that sound?"

Logan would have slumped if he had a wall to lean on, then immediately wondered if his relief was premature. Was this good news?

"I think my husband will feel a lot better about leaving the baby if we can see him first," Prissy suggested.

Yes. A good idea.

"Of course."

They followed the doctor to a nurse's station where the baby lay in a plastic bassinette. He was swaddled in a blue and white striped blanket and a tiny blue cap adorned his head.

"Oh, my stars," Prissy breathed beside him. "Logan, he is so precious."

More precious than gold.

"Mr. Shaw?" a nurse approached from down the hall. "Miss French is asking for you."

Logan hesitated. He didn't want to leave Bodie yet. Or Prissy.

"Do you want me to come with you?" she asked.

"You don't mind?"

For answer, she shook her head, and he reluctantly led the way to Cherilyn's private room. Inside, she was propped up against pillows watching television. She waved them in and muted the speaker.

"Cherilyn, this is my wife, Priscilla."

Not speaking, the younger woman inspected every inch of Prissy from her caramel striped, blond hair to her black combat boots.

If they were contestants in a beauty contest, Cherilyn would win hands-down. Even in a hospital bed, having just had surgery, she was a stunner with her golden hair and blue eyes. It was easy to see why Dummer fell for her. Yet for Logan, there was no contest; Prissy would take home the prize every time.

Cherilyn switched her gaze to him. "I'll be leaving tomorrow morning. Are you all set to take the baby home with you?"

"When he's ready."

"Good. Get him away from them, Logan. Keep him away from them."

"What's this?" Prissy asked.

"Her parents have decided they want to be part of his life now." The bitter words were dragged reluctantly from him. These were the same people who encouraged Cherilyn to hide her pregnancy from him and give the baby up for adoption.

Prissy's jaw went slack. Her doe brown eyes blinked, once, twice, then narrowed. He'd seen that stubborn look before so he wasn't surprised when she fisted her small hands at her hips and said, "This will never do."

As much as he appreciated the fight in her, for him and for Dummer's baby, he was realistic enough to understand they had legal rights too. "They are his grandparents."

Six days later he wanted to take those words back.

He and Prissy had stayed in a hotel for a couple of nights, to shower and sleep, but he couldn't be away from the restaurant indefinitely and she had shifts to work at the diner. So, they returned to Ammonoosuc Falls with the assurance that Bodie would be home in a day or two.

It turned out to be three. Though the hospital released him a day before that, he had a return appointment the very next morning and it didn't make sense for Logan to cart him all the way up I-93 and back again at such a young age. Cherilyn's parents suggested they keep him for that one night, and against his better judgement, he agreed.

They wouldn't give him back when the appointment was over.

"He has another appointment tomorrow," her mother argued.

"Makes sense," her father agreed. "No point him going all the way up there just to come down here again."

That argument matched his own reasoning, so he was leaning toward saying yes, but her mother's next words took their discussion to an entirely different level.

"We are his grandparents, after all." A title they claimed for image alone. They hadn't taken care of the baby, but hired a per diem nurse to see to his needs with the rationale that he wasn't completely out of the woods yet and a medical professional would make sure he thrived. "But, of course, if we need to formalize our rights in the courts, we can certainly do that."

This was no idle threat. He was a victim of child neglect, sometimes abuse, and he hated the court system. They knew this. Just as he knew they would take him there if he didn't go along with their proposal.

"You can come and get him on Friday for the weekend," her father offered, like it was a favor, like the baby could be put out on loan, "then bring him back on Sunday. That way he'll be close to the doctors who know him if anything goes wrong."

Logan wished Ivy were with him. Or his stubborn little wife. But he was alone and outnumbered, left with no choice but to surrender.

He finally brought Bodie home the next day.

Prissy took care of everything for him. Did he want a drink? Something to eat? Was the baby warm enough, or should she turn up the heat? She took away soiled diapers and prepared bottles of formula. She bought a baby alarm for the nursery and Logan's bedroom so he would hear Bodie if he woke.

It was a beautiful experience for him, being able to give his son all the attention he'd been unable to until now without worrying about the outside world. He watched him sleep, counting his tiny breaths and admiring the way a drop of formula pearled on his sweet lips.

This little person was completely dependent on him. For love, and nourishment, and protection. That realization filled him with awe.

Logan had loved his little brother. He had visited him every other weekend, attended his plays and sports programs, sent him gifts on his birthday and Christmas, took him for back to school shopping each year. When Dummer grew from a boy to a pre-teen, they hung out at malls and arcades. In the summer Logan took him to go-kart tracks, batting cages, and waterparks.

"I can't wait to live with you," Dummer would say each time they parted.

Logan bought Dummer a car when he got his license. This year he bought the Dunlap house for the two of them to share. They never got that chance, but Bodie would. Logan planned to give this baby all the love and security he and his brother never had.

A burst pipe in the basement at A Notch Above cut their weekend short. He called Lauren and Jamie to see if they could take Bodie, but they were down in Tyngsborough visiting her family. Ivy was on the road home from upstate New York. Chris didn't answer his phone. That left Prissy. She was working until two, but when he called Shelly said Bodie could stay in his carrier in the office. Logan left him there with instructions to Prissy about meeting Cherilyn's parents, then went to take care of the problem at the restaurant.

He was standing two feet deep in icy water when Jessie came down to the basement, phone in hand. "I think it's important," she apologized, "or I wouldn't have bothered you."

Wiping sweat and grime from his eyes, he took the phone. "Logan."

"Where are you?" Cherilyn's mother demanded.

"What's wrong?" he asked, because his location was irrelevant if Bodie was in trouble.

"Wrong? I'll tell you what's wrong. That *wife* of yours won't bring the baby back."

He didn't miss the way she couldn't even say his name—Bodie—but that took a back seat to what she had said. "Come again?" He had asked Prissy to meet them at a rendezvous point in Concord after her shift ended. "Maybe she had to work late," he thought aloud.

"No. We called to confirm the meeting place and time, and she said she wouldn't be there today or any other day."

The heat from the work light hanging behind him had nothing on the emotion roiling through his bloodstream. "I'll take care of it," he bit out, disconnecting the call.

Chapter Seventeen

Prissy knew she was in trouble when Logan's footsteps pounded across the porch and the kitchen door flew open.

She wanted to hide, like a little girl awaiting her father's censure, but this was too important. Putting Bodie in his carrier on the countertop, she took a position in front of him and waited for the storm to hit.

"What the hell are you up to?"

There it was.

"Nothing," she prevaricated. A stupid thing to do, since she knew exactly why he was here and what he was upset about. Still, she gestured to the oven behind her where a casserole was baking. "I'm just making supper."

Logan let the door swing shut behind him and advanced into the room. "You know what I mean. Why is he still here?"

"He has a name."

Probably not the smartest thing to say, unless she wanted to see steam coming out of his ears, but she was nervous.

"What. Is. Bodie. Doing. Here?"

"He's your son. This is your home. His home."

"Damnit, Prissy, this isn't a game! You were supposed to meet his grandparents in Concord and give him back. You told me you'd take care of it. Now explain to me why that didn't happen."

"They called you?"

"Of course, they called me! I was standing in two feet of water, listening to them screaming in my ear about how my *wife* won't give my kid back to them. What the hell were you thinking? Are you trying to ruin my chances at custody?"

"No."

"No?" He looked ready to explode. "That's all you have to say?"

"Yes." Her voice shook, but she stood her ground. "I'm not trying to ruin your chances, and I'm not ruining them."

"You have no idea what you're talking about."

"They are using emotional blackmail to keep you from him." She moved closer to the counter where Bodie slept beneath a light blanket, taking the carrier handle and rocking the baby back and forth. To keep him from waking, or to soothe her own nerves, she wasn't sure. "They don't deserve to have him."

"That's not your call to make. Get him ready to go."

"No."

"Come again?" he seethed, advancing on her.

She froze but didn't retreat. "I said, no, I won't get him ready."

He looked ready to throttle her, but the kitchen door opening saved her from that fate.

"Hey, I just came by to...," Ivy's voice died when she took in the two of them, facing off like they were in a boxing ring. "Am I interrupting something?"

"Thank God you're here." Logan ran his hands through his hair. "She might have just ruined my chances of permanent custody. Talk some sense into her, please. Maybe I can still call Cherilyn's parents and calm them down before it's not too late."

"What did she do?"

"They were supposed to get Bodie back after the weekend, but Prissy refused to give him to them. She didn't meet them in Concord and when they phoned, she refused to."

"*She* is right here," Prissy interjected.

Logan threw a filthy look at her.

Ivy put her purse down on the bench beside the door. "Did you refuse to return him to his grandparents, Prissy?"

"I did." Prissy's voice trembled. She couldn't read the attorney's tone, but she and Logan went way back so the odds here were not in her favor.

Ivy unbuttoned her coat and hung it on a peg. She didn't look as outraged as Logan. Maybe that was a good sign. Or maybe Prissy was looking for hope where there was none.

"Why did you refuse?"

"Because they don't care about Bodie. He deserves to be with Logan."

"That doesn't change the situation," Logan bit out.

"What makes you think they don't care about him?" Ivy asked.

"They're using him as a pawn in some game! That's not how you treat a baby, and that certainly isn't love. He's better off here with me, someone who isn't even related to him, than he is with those awful people."

Ivy's eyes widened.

Prissy fussed with Bodie's blanket to hide the tears pooling in her eyes.

Logan finally broke the silence, speaking in a slow, deliberate tone as if he was talking to a well-intentioned but naïve child. "He needs follow up care, Prissy. Specialists, to make sure he fully recovers from his respiratory infection."

"I called Kathy Schmidt." She met his gaze. "They can see him at Dartmouth."

Logan raised his eyebrows. "That was very thoughtful of you," he admitted, "but it won't keep Cherilyn's parents from coming for my jugular. They'll still claim I can't take care of him."

"I will," Prissy volunteered a little desperately.

"How, exactly, would you do that?"

"Shelly says he can stay in the kitchen as long as I have a playpen for him."

Logan ran his hands up his face, through his hair, and down the back of his neck. "What will you do?" he snapped. There was the man she knew. "Stop waiting on customers to feed him and change his diaper?"

"I don't know!" she exploded, tears spilling from her eyes. "All I know is a baby shouldn't be treated like this. He should be loved, and secure, and if that means I have to find a different job where I can take him with me, then I will, but I will not give him back to those vultures. They don't deserve him!"

Logan stumbled back at the vehemence in her voice.

Ivy smiled.

Prissy clutched the baby carrier and wept.

"Well?" Logan finally asked his cousin and attorney.

Ivy retrieved her coat and shrugged into it before replying, "She's right."

"What do you mean, right?"

"I mean, he belongs with you, and they made a mistake in using him as a prize. I can file papers for an emergency custody hearing when the courthouse opens tomorrow."

"That's a thing?"

"Just leave it to me." She opened the door and with a "Bye, Prissy," thrown over her shoulder, left them in a silent room loud with fear and anger.

Prissy stopped crying, but her trembling was so severe she had to put the baby down for fear of dropping him.

Logan stared at the closed door for several long minutes before finally turning to face her. His shoulders drooped. Fatigue settled over his features. Yet his blue gaze, when it met hers, gave nothing away. For the first time she couldn't read his emotions and it scared her more than an outburst would.

She opened her mouth to speak, then swallowed because she didn't know what to say.

"I have to finish taking care of the pipe at the restaurant."

At least he wasn't yelling at her.

He moved closer and she tensed, but he only touched a finger to Bodie's cheek and stepped away again. "You'll be okay here? You'll watch him?"

Prissy nodded.

A moment later he was gone, and she collapsed against the counter. She didn't kid herself into thinking this was over. Far from it. But without having to worry about his reaction and reassured by Ivy's plan to petition the court tomorrow morning, she could think clearly again.

They needed a plan for Bodie's care. She could give up her lunch shift to ensure that she was home before Logan left in the afternoon and someone was always with the baby, but that wasn't ideal. He sometimes worked during the day at the sand and gravel business. Shelly might let her bring Bodie in on those occasions, but a baby didn't belong in a commercial kitchen. Where else could she work, though?

Needing a distraction, she pulled the vase of flowers close and removed dead blossoms while considering her options.

Ammonoosuc Falls didn't have a daycare center. She'd have to find a job here that could accommodate Bodie or work out of town where someone else could take care of him.

No.

Bodie's mother didn't want him. His grandmother wanted him only to win against Logan. Prissy's time with him might be brief, but she would pour love into every minute and see him blossom just like the flowers in this vase.

Flowers.

"Bodie!" she exclaimed. "I've got it!"

Fifteen minutes later she removed him from his car seat and stepped inside the funeral home. "Hello?" She knew a door-activated bell chimed here and at the house to let Gil know he had visitors, but didn't know which building he was in.

"Prissy." He emerged from the office with a surprised smile on his craggy face. "What can I do for you?" He noticed Bodie in the carrier and raised his eyebrows. "And who is this?"

Life had been so crazy for the last week, she'd forgotten he didn't know about the baby. "This is Bodie. Logan's nephew, but his brother died and he's going to raise him."

Taking a breath to get her nerves under control, she said, "Did you mean it when you said you'd retire if you could find someone to take over the business for you?"

"Yes. Why, do you know someone who's interested?"

"I am." Once the words were out of her mouth, she felt almost dizzy with relief.

"You are?"

The idea had been spontaneous, but the more it rolled around inside her head during the drive here, the more certain she was. Four years of college and two years of medical school were behind her. She loved science. She liked making people feel good. What could be more natural than for her to put that combination to work in a funeral home.

"I am," she repeated. "If you would be open to having an apprentice? If that's even a thing? And could the baby stay in a playpen when I'm here?"

"Why don't we sit down and talk about it?"

She could apprentice with a funeral home director in New Hampshire, but there were forms to fill out and an application to complete. Gil suggested she spend afternoons training with him and said that yes, Bodie could accompany her, but once he started walking, they'd have to revisit that idea.

Prissy didn't tell him she might not be part of the baby's life by then. As far as Gil knew, she was a newlywed with a long marriage ahead of her.

"Do you have Wednesday off this week?"

She nodded.

"Why don't we meet then? Say, one o'clock?"

"Perfect. Thank you so much. I'll make sure you don't regret this."

Would she? Prissy wasn't normally an impulsive person. That seemed to have changed since coming to Ammonoosuc Falls. Maybe it was just that desperate circumstances made her act out of character. Whatever the reason, she had jumped in feet first, and now it was time to think about her idea from a practical standpoint.

Tomorrow she would ask Shelly about giving up or reducing her lunch shifts. Bodie could stay with Logan in the mornings and she could pick him up between jobs. Assuming he would agree to that.

Their marriage contract was for six months, but there was no stipulation that she had to leave the area after their divorce. Maybe he would let her be Bodie's stepmother and have some role in his life.

Before she could start crying again at the thought of that future separation, she tucked the baby into his bassinette, took a seat in the rocking chair, and dialed her parents' number.

The phone rang once, and she tensed. She hated asking for their help. Another ring. She considered ending the call before it connected. They had done so much for her, and she didn't want to burden them with her worries. She was proud of her ability to solve her own problems. Another ring. One more and the recording would come on. It was a Sunday night. Maybe they had gone to the evening church service, and she should just leave a message.

"Prissy?"

Hearing her mother's voice, she took a deep breath. For Logan, and Bodie, she would swallow her pride and ask for their support.

"Mom? I need help."

Across town, Logan had gathered his friends at A Notch Above for similar reasons. He had just finished explaining what went down between Prissy and Cherilyn's parents.

Chris was the first to speak. "Well, damn."

"I know." Logan lifted a glass tumbler to his lips, needing the whiskey's kick after the day he had. When he drained the glass to ice, he put it down on the table. "Pretty ballsy, right?"

"I guess she's not so ditzy after all."

"What are you talking about?"

"I mean, when has a woman ever stood up for you in your life, man? And here you have one, who isn't even staying into summer, and she's going to the wall for you and your kid."

Surprised, Logan said, "You sound like you admire her."

Chris shrugged.

"And what about you?" Until now, Jamie hadn't given an opinion.

"I'm with him. She's good for you."

"You mean she's good for my chances at getting custody," Logan clarified.

"No, brother. She's good for you."

"People in town like her," Chris pointed out.

"She's comfortable in our world," Jamie added.

"Our world?"

"You know, local boys made good."

Logan almost smiled at the description.

"She's not a snob about our roots."

"She's not after you for your money."

At Logan's raised eyebrows, they all chuckled.

"Okay, so she was after money," Chris conceded, "but it's not exactly yours, and she didn't lie about it."

"She slings hash in the morning and talks to Ivy League professors at night," Jamie continued, echoing Logan's own assessment not so long ago.

"And Ivy says she was right about the kid," Chris reminded him. "That's got to count for something."

"Let her help you, brother."

He drove home with those words echoing in his mind.

The outside light was on, but the interior was dark. In a weird replay of another night, he used his cellphone to navigate the stairs and checked each room for Prissy. He found her curled up in her sleeping bag on the floor beside Bodie's bassinet, reminding him of the weeks she spent sleeping on the other side of the bedroom at his apartment.

She had never complained. Muffy was right about that.

Backing out so he wouldn't wake her, he returned to his room and sat on the edge of the mattress, palming his cell phone. Prissy was in his corner. He had Ivy on his side. There was only one woman left whose help he needed to win this custody battle. He dialed her number, and she answered on the second ring. "Logan?"

"Cherilyn. We need to talk about your parents."

Chapter Eighteen

Prissy lived the next three weeks in a state of emotional suspense. Logan was granted a stay by the court, which meant Cherilyn's parents couldn't take any action until a formal hearing was held, but until then their lives were a roller coaster of hope and anxiety.

Logan watched Bodie in the mornings. If she was on schedule for lunch, he brought him to the diner before going to the restaurant. Twice a week she came home after breakfast and took him with her to the funeral home.

She cherished her time alone with the baby. Whether she was giving him his bath, rocking him to sleep with a lullaby, or merely standing over his bassinette watching him breathe, she burned those sweet moments into her memory.

The hardest times were watching Logan do the same. He held Bodie as if he was more precious than air, running the tip of his finger along the baby's nose, cheek, or the shell of his ear. He held him long after they were both asleep, when Prissy would slip her fingers beneath his and carry the baby to his bassinette.

Sometimes they would both be up with late night feedings and talk in hushed voices while watching over Bodie.

"My mother sold herself," Logan admitted one night out of the blue.

Prissy made no reply, afraid he would stop if she did. This was the first time he had volunteered anything about his life without being asked.

"She wasn't on a street corner—" his laugh was humorless — "as if there is any traffic around here, but she went from bed to bed and man to man for whatever she could get from them. Grocery money, rent, oil."

"That's why you reacted the way you did when I made my offer."

"Your bribe."

She waved her hand in a whatever motion, not offended because he had said it with a smile.

"I was pretty bad to you that night."

"You had just lost your brother. I understand now."

A deep sigh came from the corner of the room where he sat beside the bassinette.

"Was Dummer unhappy? In his foster home?"

"No." Logan shook his head. "They were good people."

A few nights later it was her turn to open up. "I had cancer when I was a girl."

"Your family told me."

"They did everything for me, Logan. Muffy was barely out of diapers, Dad had just bought another business. I didn't understand then how much they were dealing with, but now..."

"It was bad?"

"Mom stopped working, Dad sold off his small engine shop and farm equipment rental place-that was his newest acquisition-and we were on the road all the time, seeing doctors and going for treatments. Sometimes they would talk about money, when they thought I was asleep in the back seat."

"Were you scared?"

"Some. Mostly when I couldn't talk, but I knew my family would take care of me."

A high moon breached the window frame and shone a path across the room to where he sat in the rocking chair. He was so handsome, and strong, she wanted to help him through this in any way she could. Take care of him, the way her loved ones had taken care of her.

"That's why you don't spend money?"

"Hmm. I'd already cost them so much. I learned to sew to make my own clothes. I worked weekends and after school. When it was time for college, I applied for every scholarship I could get my hands on, but I still had to take out loans."

"They wouldn't want you to live in poverty, Prissy."

"I know. But I wouldn't want them to, either."

The court date arrived in the middle of a week plagued by ice storms. Logan had once asked her what she knew about that particular weather condition. She'd had no clue it could be this bad and was terrified to walk from the house to the truck.

"Are you sure it's safe to go out in this?" She stood on the kitchen doorstep, eyeing the six feet of space between herself and his vehicle. The engine was running, the windows de-iced, but she could slip and die before she got there.

"Just keep your feet on the sand and you'll be fine."

He carried Bodie while she picked her way across the gravel path he had laid down.

Once she was safely inside the vehicle, he returned to grab Bodie's bag and she took that moment to say her farewells to the baby because, even if Logan won the custody battle, she would be out of their lives by summer.

"Do you know how much I love you?" she whispered to the little bundle whose future lay in the balance. Footsteps crunched across the ice and Logan passed in front of the truck on his way to the driver's side. "I love you more than rainbows." She wasn't speaking only to the baby.

The drive to the county buildings on Route 10 was hairy.

"Are you sure Ivy will be there?" she asked when they had to slow to twenty miles below the speed limit.

"It's almost a straight shot from her apartment here, once she's on the main road. She'll be there."

A few minutes later his phone buzzed. He put it on speaker, and they listened to Chris explain that several smaller roads were still blocked by fallen trees and downed wires. He and Jamie were working with the fire department to clean them up, but they might not be able to make it before their case was heard.

She and Logan arrived at the modern brick and glass building with the blue state seal on the wall a few minutes ahead of schedule despite the driving conditions.

"This is it?" Prissy whispered.

When Logan didn't answer, she glanced over to see him gripping the steering wheel, perspiration beading on his forehead. "Are you okay?"

"No." A guttural reply, like the cry of a wounded animal.

"Hey," Prissy reached out and placed her hand on his forearm, finding it rigid. "Ivy said we don't have anything to worry about."

"Where is she?" He scanned the parking lot with wild eyes. His lawyer/friend/cousin was four feet in front of their vehicle, waiting for them, but he didn't see her. He was, literally, blinded by fear.

"Logan, look at me."

He met her gaze, but she wasn't sure he saw her at all.

"Take a deep breath."

He inhaled, made a choking sound. All the color leached from his face.

Prissy was starting to panic herself now. Where was her normally strong, confident husband? She wanted to reach across the truck cab and hug him, but Bodie slept between them in his car seat, so she had to settle for stroking his arm.

"Talk to me," she encouraged. "What's this all about?"

"I've been here before."

"Okay," she soothed. "When you were younger?"

He nodded. "As soon as I turned eighteen, I came for custody of Dummer. The judge wouldn't give him to me."

His adam's apple bobbed and he stopped speaking.

"You're no longer eighteen."

"No." He shook his head as if to clear it and finally let go of the steering wheel. "I tried again when I was twenty-two. Same result."

All she could think to say was, "You're no longer twenty-two."

"Yes." A heavy breath gusted out of him, fogging up the driver's side window.

"You own a home, a business, and you're married now."

He sank back against the driver's seat and finally looked at her. "Thank you."

A knock on his window made them both jump. "Let's go rout this beast!" Ivy shouted through the glass.

They followed her into the building, but with each step Prissy grew more nervous. It was one thing to tell Logan everything would be fine, another to believe it. What did she know about courts and custody battles?

Cherilyn's parents were already inside. She and Logan sat on the other side of the room.

Minutes ticked by. Hushed conversations seemed magnified. Each time the doors opened, Prissy swung around to see who came in, deflating with every stranger who entered.

"You're not helping me," Logan muttered.

She forced herself to sit still.

"Mr. Shaw?" A court employee approached them, and at Logan's nod, said, "Could you come with me? The judge would like to speak with you."

Logan's face drained of color, but he rose and followed the man. Prissy glanced at Ivy. "It's okay," she said, "Judges often talk to the parties separately. Sometimes they give them a room to meet in, to see if they can reach an agreement on their own."

Prissy relaxed slightly, tensing again when the doors behind her opened again. This time she resisted the urge to look.

"It's Jamie."

He and Lauren settled into seats behind them, followed a few minutes later by Chris, then Gil. Prissy started crying when her friend reached over the back of the seat and squeezed her shoulder. He handed her a tissue.

"You must own stock in Kleenex," she joked, the moment of levity allowing her to pull herself together only to start up again when Shelly joined them.

LOGAN ALMOST STUMBLED back into the courtroom, wanting to throw up, wanting to tell Prissy what happened, but they called for her before he had a chance to. She returned a few minutes later, face drained of color, rushed over and all but threw herself against him.

He had no time to do anything but catch her.

"All rise."

"Please be seated."

Beside him, Prissy trembled.

"...French vs. Shaw...please rise."

Logan fumbled for her hand. Her grip was as desperate as his.

"You are Mr. and Mrs. French?" the judge asked of Cherilyn's parents.

"We are, your honor."

Logan's gaze swung to the judge. They were a polished, attractive, polite couple. As phony as two people could be, yet they presented themselves as caring when the situation called for it.

"And you are Mr. and Mrs. Shaw?"

He and Prissy confirmed it for the record.

"Mr. and Mrs. French, I've read your complaint. You wish to have sole custody of your grandchild, Bodie Dunlap Shaw, is that correct?"

"Yes, your honor," they chorused.

"Explain why you think you would be the best choice, and not his uncle."

They started with his background, saying that he had been in some trouble as a teenager and because he grew up in a non-traditional setting, he wouldn't know how to provide one for Bodie. They were smart about it, acknowledging his success since then and his notable commitment to his late brother. Then they added their caveat. His marriage was false, arranged solely for the purpose of this hearing, and wouldn't last once custody of Bodie was secure.

"And the baby's mother?"

As if she heard the question, Cherilyn came through the doors at the back of the room and hurried up the aisle. "Sorry I'm late. Trees down on the road. I had to find another way around."

"Who are you?" the judge asked.

"I'm the baby's birth mother, Cherilyn French," she answered, glancing at Logan before asking, "Is it our turn already?"

"Ahem." The judge waited until he had her attention and order in the court. "Are you here to speak to this custody dispute?"

"I am, your honor."

"Please take a seat until I call on you."

Logan heard every word of the exchange that followed, but if anyone asked later what was said, he wouldn't be able to repeat a single part of it. This wasn't just stress. This was terror, debilitating, sick to the stomach, fear of losing his child terror.

Cherilyn's parents said they had interviewed people in town and learned that he and Prissy made some temporary deal, just so he could get custody of the baby. The judge ruled that out as hearsay and turned to Logan.

"Is this a real marriage, or a marriage of convenience?"

Logan swallowed the bile rising in his throat. Perspiration coated his forehead. Coming to court, any court, for any reason, was enough to make him lose his breakfast

It was one thing to answer the judge's question in the privacy of that back room, which he had done, but to be asked the same thing in front of everyone in the courthouse put his reputation in jeopardy. When word got out, people might never look at him the same way. Worse, he could lose his child for admitting what they'd done.

He glanced at Prissy. Tears matted her eyelashes, her fearful gaze continually going to Bodie where he slept in his carrier. The truth coming out would hurt her as much as him, yet he turned back to the judge and gave the same answer he had given in chambers, "Yes, sir, our marriage started out as a crazy deal that would help me if a custody dispute ever came about."

Murmurs came from someone seated behind them. Cherilyn's parents smiled. Prissy's small hand squeezed his fingers tighter and she whispered, "You didn't have to say that. I would have backed you up if you lied."

He didn't get a chance to reply, because the judge fixed her with a stern look and said, "And you, Mrs. Shaw, you admit to this as well?"

Prissy shook so much Logan wrapped his arm around her shoulder and pulled her to his side to keep her upright.

"It was all my idea," she said in her wispy little voice. Her taking responsibility for their marriage didn't surprise him, but her next words did, "I needed the money from the reality show I was in, and I could only get it if I married someone local."

"I see." The judge's tone was void of emotion. "And you agreed to share this money with your husband?"

"I promised to give him half."

"You see, your honor—"

Cherilyn's mother stopped talking when the judge raised his hand for silence. "Mrs. Shaw, you say this money was important to you. Why is that?"

"I went to medical school and have huge student loans. I planned to pay them down with that money."

"Planned to? Has something changed?"

Prissy glanced at Logan, but he couldn't read her expression before she returned her attention to the judge. "If it helps Logan's case, your honor, the show can keep the money."

Logan jerked. Bodie blinked his eyes awake. The judge turned to the other side of the aisle. "Miss French, could you please come to the microphone."

Cherilyn moved forward.

"Who do you think your son should live with?"

"Logan and his wife."

Her parents gasped. "Be honest," she said over her shoulder to them. "You don't really want to spend the next eighteen years raising another child."

"Ahem." The judge clearing his throat stopped her parents from answering.

"Your honor, the baby's father loved Logan more than anyone else in the world. More than me, and I know he loved me." Cherilyn sniffed, wiped her eyes, and continued. "He talked about him all the time, about what a great big brother he was, and how he couldn't wait to live with him. He wanted Logan to raise his child for him."

"And what would you recommend for visiting rights? For your parents, I mean, if I should grant custody to Mr. and Mrs. Shaw."

Prissy tensed. Logan stopped breathing.

"I think they can work something out, when the baby is older, but my parents work long hours, and they travel a lot. Logan owns a restaurant and is out at night, but if that baby needs him at home, I know he'll be there for him."

The judge seemed to ponder her statement for a moment, before saying, "I've met with most of you individually, and I believe the best place for young Bodie is right where he is. The circumstances of this marriage are irrelevant, because it is real now. They have a home, have made room in that home for a child, and from what I can see they both love him unconditionally. Mr. and Mrs. French, you tried to impose conditions on parenthood for them, which I find reprehensible. However, I recognize that a child needs his grandparents as well. Reasonable visitation for you will be arranged at Mr. and Mrs. French's discretion. I have also received a certified letter from a Mr. and Mrs. Schermerhorn of Florida, who claim to be Mrs. Shaw's parents. Is that right?"

Prissy nodded, then remembering to speak for the record, said, "Yes, sir."

"They sent this in case the weather interfered with their ability to be here." Everyone looked around as if they could see the wintry conditions through the paneled walls. "The Schermerhorns plan to be as active as grandparents can be from a distance and promise to visit each year. Specifically, they say that any child of Priscilla and Logan is a grandchild of theirs."

Prissy's shoulders convulsed and she leaned into Logan's side. He was the one trembling now, waiting desperately for the judge's next words.

"So, it would seem this baby has a lot of people fighting for him. Good luck to you all."

The sun came out. Literally, they walked out of the courthouse to a changed environment. Gone was the gloom that had hovered over the region for three days, a golden glow melting layers of ice from every surface.

"Well, what now?" Ivy asked when they were gathered around Logan's truck. "Party?"

He looked at his wife, almost wilting at his side, looked at Bodie who was wide awake but unaware, and said, "Now we're going home."

They crashed on the couch as soon as they were inside.

Hours later, his phone ringing woke him to a cool living room and a crick in his neck. Bodie was asleep against his shoulder. Prissy lay curled up beneath the throw blanket.

Logan blinked and brought the number into focus before answering, "Yeah, what's up?"

"Trouble at the common," Chris said. "We need you here."

"What? Now?" What kind of trouble could there be?

As if he asked the question allowed, Chris said, "We need all hands on deck. Bring Prissy, too."

The call ended.

"Who was it?" Prissy's soft voice asked.

"Chris. He said we've got to get to the common."

"What for?"

"Your guess is as good as mine." Yet his friend had sounded anxious on the phone, and since Chris was a trained volunteer firefighter, it must be something big. He and Prissy loaded up the baby and headed for town.

Several cars were parked around the common. He couldn't see any emergency, but the number of people milling on the green, now patches of snow, ice, and open ground, was significant. Lights were on inside the covered bridge. He found a place to park along the rim road and helped Prissy out of the truck.

Chris broke free of the crowd and came to greet them.

"Good to see you, buddy." He clapped Logan on the shoulder. "We've got something going on inside the bridge."

Still confused, Logan nonetheless took Prissy's elbow with one hand and Bodie's carrier with the other.

A few feet from the bridge opening they stopped on seeing a blue and white banner draped across the entrance, "Congratulations!"

spelled out on the shiny fabric in giant silver letters. Blue and white balloons festooned the railings, drawing his eye to the long table inside draped with blue cloth and covered by a mound of wrapped gifts.

Lauren came toward them, hands patting little Chris in his sling at her front. "It's your baby shower," she explained. "Everyone who couldn't get through to the courthouse came here instead and set this up."

"Say thank you," Lulu encouraged.

Logan was so surprised by everything, he hadn't noticed his sister-in laws in the crowd. Beside Lulu, Muffy stamped her feet impatiently and said, "C'mon, big brother, let's get this show on the road. It's cold out here!"

Her sisters, co-workers, his restaurant staff, folks from local businesses, they were all here to celebrate with them. While he absorbed this, her parents arrived, giving him a moment alone with Prissy while her sisters helped carry their gifts from a rental car to the table.

"Did you know about this?"

"Me? No."

He looked out over the common, trying to come up with words for what was roiling through him. So many emotions, so few words.

"Can I stay, Logan?"

He didn't dare breathe. Had he heard her correctly? Had she really said the words he'd waited his whole life to hear?

She pressed against his side, hope and heart shining in her soft brown eyes, and though he wanted nothing more than to pull her close, and keep her close, he had to let her speak because he couldn't afford to be wrong about this. "What are you asking?"

"When the six months is up, do I have to go?" Her beautiful lips trembled, and a tear fell onto her cheek. "I'll understand if you say no—"

He covered her mouth with his own. A hard, dry, kiss that made her eyes go wide and left her silent when he pulled his head back. "Are you trying to renegotiate our agreement, Priscilla Daphne Nicole Schermerhorn Shaw?"

She nodded. "Guilty."

"I think I've learned a few things about bargaining," he said.

"Oh?" A smile hovered on her lips. "From anyone special?"

"The most special person I know." He kissed her again. "But, Prissy?"

"Hmm?"

"There will be no expiration date. This contract is for the rest of our lives."

THE END

Don't miss out!

Visit the website below and you can sign up to receive emails whenever Amber Cross publishes a new book. There's no charge and no obligation.

https://books2read.com/r/B-A-NVSCB-WFSBF

BOOKS 2 READ

Connecting independent readers to independent writers.

Did you love *The Marriage Bribe*? Then you should read *The Light at Corriveau Crossing*[1] by Amber Cross!

Levi Turner ran from northern Maine thirteen years ago, and he wouldn't be back now if his father didn't need him. He'll stay just long enough to see the man on his feet and do his best to avoid Carissa Michaud while he's there.

Easier said than done. Carissa throws down on him the very first night. She accuses him of abandoning his family; he challenges her rose-colored view of their childhood. They spar more often than talk, but when a child goes missing in the Great North Woods and they team up to find her, their relationship starts to change.

Levi recognizes the caring behind her nosy behavior and develops an appreciation for her unflagging honesty. Carissa had thought his

---

1. https://books2read.com/u/bMnLjX

2. https://books2read.com/u/bMnLjX

close-mouthed, often surly manner meant he didn't care. Now she realizes the opposite is true.

Yet the clock is ticking. His life is in North Carolina, hers in Maine. Their inevitable parting is full of harsh words and hurt feelings. Levi can't tell her he might be back because he doesn't want to get her hopes up and disappoint her. Carissa is not too proud to tell him how she feels, but she is too proud to ask him to stay. His mother says living in their wild pocket of woodland makes some people crazy, while it calls to others.

It's not the land calling him; it's the woman.

Read more at https://www.amber-cross.com.

Also by Amber Cross

A Covered Bridge Romance
The Marriage Bribe

Love in the Kingdom
Precedent for Passion

Standalone
Her Wild Defender
The Light at Corriveau Crossing

Watch for more at https://www.amber-cross.com.

About the Author

Amber Cross was raised on a family farm in New England, one of a dozen siblings, each one inspiring my writing in some way. I still live in that same small town with my husband and the youngest of our five children. I love spending time in the woods, in the water, and watching people because every one of them has a unique and fascinating story to tell.

Read more at https://www.amber-cross.com.